THE JASMINE NEGATIVE

Novels by Dennis Bowen

International Thriller Series

THE WATER DIAMONDS
Book 1

THE BLACKSTONE PERFECTION
Book 2

THE CRYSTAL SEDUCTION
Book 3

THE REDROCK QUARANTINE
Book 4

THE FINAL MASQUERADE
Book 5

THE VIRTUE TRANSITION
Book 6

THE JASMINE NEGATIVE
Book 7

The Backstory Files

STONES
Book 1

THE JASMINE NEGATIVE

Dennis Bowen

The Jasmine Negative is a work of fiction. Names, characters, places, and incidents are the products of the author's imagination or are used fictitiously. Any resemblance to actual events, locales, or persons, living or dead, is entirely coincidental.

ISBN: 978-1-7325610-5-2

www.facebook.com/DennisBowenThrillers

www.twitter.com/DBowenThrillers

www.DennisBowen.com

Book Interior Design by 52 Novels

ACKNOWLEDGMENTS

Thank you to the readers who have immersed themselves in my *International Thriller Series*. While I create the intrigues that span the globe and enjoy every minute of it, in the end, I write these novels for you and your enjoyment, it's that simple.

As with *The Water Diamonds, The Blackstone Perfection*, *The Crystal Seduction*, *The Redrock Quarantine, The Final Masquerade,* and *The Virtue Transition,* my appreciation and gratitude goes out to those who offered suggestions and encouragement during the writing of *The Jasmine Negative.*

I express appreciation to my fabulous editor, Laura Taylor. She has provided the editing prowess to insure a quality presentation for this series and for STONES of *The Backstory Files.*

As in life, each successive endeavor—such as writing a series of novels—is built on what came before. Any errors or omissions in *The Jasmine Negative* I claim as my own.

Once again, I extend my gratitude to family members and friends for their support, and to former colleagues, some of whom offered up their lives in the service of this great country, and whose presence in my life gives my International Thriller Series its noted sense of reality. Thank you to all.

—Dennis Bowen

CHAPTER 1

The two couples, two-thirds of the Crayle team, sat together. The sofa of the restored Crayle cabin accommodated them and provided a magnificent view of the lake as they recounted their Ulurú experiences. In Australia.

"That was hilarious, Mag," Micmac said. "When the three bombs had gone off at the Aussie's mines in the distance, and the babies started coming."

"I thought I handled the modicum of stress rather well."

"Absolutely. No panic at all. I remember your dulcet tones. Something like the following. *'Micmac! Tell me you know what to do!'*"

Hekka's lips formed into one of her minimalist smiles.

Magus Crayle's long time compatriot and friend clasped his wife's hand.

Phoebe squeezed her husband's hand back.

"You weren't done. Then, you yelled out... *'Micmac! You were a Navy SEAL, for Chrissakes!'*"

They laughed so hard, they all grabbed their bellies.

A few minutes of that, and Crayle once again took the lead. "I'll put on some dance music." He stood. "Help me move stuff out of the way."

They pushed back the sofa, set the coffee table to one side, and then rolled up the rug to reveal an oak-planked floor.

"Perfect." Crayle fetched a remote control from the coffee table.

"A little Duke Ellington from before our time."

The two couples engaged and moved quite unlike an assemblage of international spies. Then a slow dance. Each pair embraced, moving to the music and the warmth generated by the close contact. Romantic.

A huge jolt knocked all four to the floor.

Quick, they picked themselves up, all recalling that they *were* in Southern California.

Crayle observed the obvious. "That old San Andreas Fault is active again."

From the distance, the sound of an incredible blast struck their ears.

The double-paned and bullet proof windows bowed in and out.

Then, another blast. Not near. But just as loud.

Back onto the floor.

They crawled to the back door, slid it open, and caught a glimpse.

A scan left to the east yielded nothing. They checked the other direction.

"Look." Hekka pointed over the mountains that bordered the west end of Big Bear Lake.

Over those hills, the head of a mushroom cloud pushed skyward. Moments later, a second.

"Oh, God! Atomic. And that's where Los Angeles makes its home."

"Or used to."

Then, two more similar explosions. Each closer than the previous.

The ground convulsed again.

"In the car! Now!" Crayle yelled.

They ran at full speed to the garage, yanked the parachute cover from the Cobra, and all four piled in, and on.

"Somebody's marching them our way!"

In the driver's seat, Crayle spun the visceral sports car out of the driveway and onto North Shore Drive. Headed east. Headed away.

Up through the gears. Eighty miles per hour. One hundred. A hundred twenty.

"If I'm right…" Crayle advised. "… there'll be one more!"

• • •

The first bomb struck at 7:30 a.m. Getting to work in metro L.A. during morning rush hour repeated each day, each week, and so on with very little diversion from the norm. Thousands of cars, trucks, buses, and motorcycles performed daily like multitudinous streams of ants, each following the one in front. Those who didn't survive the commute found themselves carted off to the side like battlefield casualties.

Those who smuggled the first bomb into the Queen Mary, now a hotel in Long Beach, also smuggled a quite similar device onto the Queen Mary 2 just months earlier. With exceptional skill sets and otherworldly good fortune, the Crayle team thwarted the attempt by the Elder's Illuminé secret society to blow up New York City.

Choosing the archived, original Queen seemed symbolic.

As commonplace as severe tragedies had become in the world during the Crayle period, it was small wonder the media types overcame any semblance of journalistic standards, and had an all out mêlée to see who could outdo the tabloids, and each other, by the greatest margin. The following was one of the more egregious examples:

> *Like a giant carpet stretched north, south, and east, the land on which L.A. resided undulated as the Mary exploded into shards of molten hull iron, anchors, glass, and turned to vapor*

those who enjoyed what they believed to be a quiet hotel night aboard her away from home.

In the first instant, the brute force of the nuclear explosion struck the 405 Freeway segments and twenty-six miles west to Catalina Island. The freeways, much of them suspended and wrapped around like steel reinforced pretzels, splintered in places, causing them to whip through the air like snakes.

Vehicles by the thousands were flung in all directions, many into the skyscrapers of the multitude of cities comprising metropolitan L.A.

Blowing away from shore, the blast caught three cruise ships headed out to sea. It crammed their noses into the roil of the Pacific and yanked free their rudders and screws. The latter, spinning at an insane rate of speed, blew west of the epicenter, cutting a swath through railroads, motor boats, and all else before bouncing up and cutting grooves through rich and poor residential districts alike.

*L.A. was flattened like a steamroller crushing a vast extent of Tinker Toys and Legos. The hurricane force winds slammed into the Santa Monica Mountains, turning the famed **HOLLYWOOD** sign to creamy dust.*

On the east side of the city, in the enclosed spaces of Disneyland's Pirates of the Caribbean, a vehicle had just commenced its slide at a very steep angle in the dark, heading for the much anticipated wet plunge at the bottom. Just as the riders readied for the impact, the second nuclear bomb struck. The cataclysmic force redefined the excitement typically rendered by the venerable E-Ticket.

At five megatons, all of the Disney property, all of surrounding Anaheim, and all other boroughs turned to molten goo.

Instead of cancelling each other as the bomb blasts clashed, they seemed to gather steam as the multiplied force moved east.

CHAPTER 2

As the Crayles and MacKays hit the exit for Highway 18 north, it happened.

Bomb number five struck high above the Lake Arrowhead resort just west of the Big Bear Valley. Apparently, some of the Crayle team's enemies misunderstood the directions and targeted the other of the two mountain resorts.

The hills and dales of the mountain valleys, with their nooks and crannies, helped to dissipate the massive intensity only a bit.

The aggregation of hurricane force winds from five smallish, sequential nuclear detonations swung the Cobra from side to side as it snaked downhill on the already treacherous two-lane road.

With Micmac in the passenger seat and Crayle driving, Hekka and Phoebe lay sprawled atop the trunk, their arms wrapped around the two roll hoops.

The full force of the highly compressed front of air slammed them as the 18 straightened out at the mountainside bottom.

The Cobra spun like a pinwheel as it slid sideways into the lot of the gravel quarry, skidding to a stop just outside the special garage. The one the workers never used. The one that provided access to the CIA's covert hospital deep underground.

Crayle entered the special code. The garage door opened. He drove inside. The door closed behind. The vehicle elevator started them down.

"Oh!" Hekka cried.

"OMG!" cried Phoebe.

Crayle and Micmac spun to their wives, reassuring them.

"We're safe! We made it!" they exclaimed in unison.

"No," the women chorused. "It's not that! Lenny! Alona! They have our babies! Go back!"

"There is no back. Not with that last blast."

The sounds of their anguish followed them as the elevator descended three hundred feet at express speed.

At the bottom, a smiling, but deeply agitated Doctor Rorschach greeted them in his Swiss-English dialect reserved for stress situations. "How vas de shaker vee chust hat? Hmmm?"

"No shaker, Doc. Five nukes."

"Oh! I . . . I . . ."

Crayle interrupted the word-deprived doctor. "Doc! The ladies! Recently had babies! Fragile!"

The CIA's primary research psychiatrist's skin bleached more pale than the pristine hospital walls. He raised his wrist. "Mine eye-vatch!"

He tapped it. Then spoke a keyword.

A low volume siren sounded. Orderlies and nurses ran out of their rooms like keystone cops.

Crayle tried to reassure. "You sure know how to initiate a panic, Doc. The bombs were evenly spaced in time. The time lapse after the fifth one implies that what we've experienced seems to be the lot of them. The good news? Whoever set them off must think we're dead."

Seconds later, one of the hospital's windows, which appeared to depict a bright Fall day outside, changed. A split-screen briefing from the CIA's temporary Manassas headquarters began. They saw their boss, Jack Sommers, on the right, devastation footage on the left.

"Très ugly, guys. Worse than you can imagine, per the media. Stay safe. I'm CIA Central these days, and we just got real busy. Sorry I can't cuss and discuss. Expect a call from the president. Gotta go." He rang off.

The high definition display reverted to its window incarnation.

Autumn.

Birds chirping.

The satellite videos Rorschach just witnessed, and the violent shaking that bounced his research patients from their beds and pitched a plethora of items from the shelves, brought the situation home to the doctor and to his new guests.

The women, perhaps two of the strongest on the planet, descended into hysteria regarding the loss of their newborns.

The two men seated themselves on the floor, their backs to the wall. Unable to speak. Catatonic.

Crayle's phone rang. A specific ring tone he thought he'd never hear again.

His fingers fumbled on Answer and Speaker in rapid succession.

"Jeez-Louise! That was one hell of an earthquake," echoed across the room.

"Lenny?"

"What?"

"Where the … never mind." Crayle gasped out a breath.

"We decided to trek the seventy miles north today. Here we are at the water park up past Barstow, and just now got the kids into the water. They're having a blast."

"A blast? You don't know, do you?"

"Know what? We left Big Bear early this morning and plowed through miles of fog. All the way across the high desert. It was awful. Can't see anything. Still."

"Lenny, it wasn't an earthquake. It was nukes. L.A. hit first. Then, four more. Last one, Arrowhead."

"C'mon, you guys. I like a joke as much as the next asshole. But I'm not buying any of this nuke crap. Why, down in New Zealand and Australia, they have me as an expert on the subject. After I saved their big rugby game from the Illuminé bad guy's mini-nuke."

"Listen up. Jack gave us a briefing. Just minutes ago. Devastation from the coast all the way to Big Bear. Don't know about our homes, but it looks real bad. We made it to the Quarry. Just. All four. Safe. For now."

Lenny waxed silent for seconds as he digested the reality. "I don't suppose you have any good news."

"Only one thing."

"And..."

"Jack says that there was no detection of radiation fallout from any of the blasts. Otherwise, the whole Los Angeles basin and all the way out to San Bernardino and environs would be uninhabitable for any of our lifetimes and beyond."

"I suppose I should buy some Home Depot stock."

"Just a second. Hekka and Phoebe want to say something." He handed his phone to the women, who'd sufficiently calmed to process the entire conversation.

Phoebe choked out, "Lenny, God bless you and Alona. We thought... never mind what we thought. I forgive you for everything."

Lenny checked his phone for processing errors.

"Put our babies on. Please."

The former private investigator engaged his cell phone camera and streamed the tiny kids splashing gleefully in a shallow water pond. Watching them, about twenty feet away, Alona had heard none of the conversation.

"Who is it, Lenny?" she said. "Anyone we know?"

She saw the serious look on his face. One she'd had a great deal of practice getting to know. Her assessment took seconds.

"What's happened?"

• • •

Kimbel Stones possessed many positive attributes, but not patience. When his aide fumbled a speed dial input, he reached for the presidential Smartphone, but suffered a rebuke.

"Sorry, Mr. President. Protocol. It has to be me."

"And if you are somehow killed, say, by a president gone ape shit?"

The much younger man sighed in relief. "There! Ape shit avoided!"

The red iPhone rang.

"We're at the Quarry," it answered. "They didn't get us."

"You're 300 feet below ground. How the hell is your phone working? Never mind. Who's with you?"

Crayle told him.

"Thank God. But what's this *didn't get us* shit? I was briefed right away. The attack was on L.A."

"It's simple, Kimbel. Whoever it is decided to walk the bombs in like artillery. From the coast. There's symbolism in it. I just don't know what it is. Not yet."

"I'm confident your mind will get there in time, if you live long enough. I'm sorry. I didn't mean … "

"Mr. President … Kimbel. Jack said no radiation was released."

"Oh, crap. I see where you're going."

Crayle heard him ask his aide.

"None. Good for the folks who survived. And the place remains re-inhabitable. But you and I both know what this means."

"Every one of those nukes had Made In China stamped on it."

"The young empress has some splainin' to do."

"I'll call her when we're done."

"It comes down to this. The nuke factory of the young empress you know so well has to go. Get it done, Mag. No matter what it takes. Get it done."

Stones rang off.

The implications of the president's order rang crystal clear. They played into Crayle's mind as much as they struck his heart. The mini-nukes built and sold under the Chin Yao-wu label either had remnants no one knew about or worse. They were still being concocted with Ling's full knowledge and approval. The factory had to go. The supply lines had to go. All remaining customers had to be identified and taken out. A potentially huge undertaking.

Because such an op would be classified far above Top Secret. The magnitude of it all might even require a new security compartment. Perhaps, USI. *Ultra Sensitive Information.*

The succinct order from the president meant for Crayle to traipse the globe and shut everything down utilizing just his six member team. Not even Micmac's crew of retired SEAL Team Sixers or Hekka's pair of 101st Airborne Screaming Eagles brothers could be accessed for this one.

And Ling. What of her? The transference of guilt for massive death and destruction beyond the perpetrator of the explosions to her was unavoidable and inevitable. The whole issue could be what Ling's short but desperate-to-talk voice message had been about.

For sure, there would be no making of deals. And he couldn't delegate this one. He'd have to take her out personally.

He was jarred to consciousness by his phone. One of his few special ring tones. He answered. It was her.

"Hello, Ling. I was just thinking of you. Are you all right?"

"A recent little skirmish with Yellow."

"Tell me."

She informed him of the attempt on her life. The poisoned cup of tea. "I utilized my Death Touch skills."

Crayle couldn't believe what he'd just heard.

"Oh, my God. You killed Yellow?"

"It needed to be done. But I couldn't. Living together as adopted sisters to each other. I couldn't. I used the milder form of the Death Touch techniques to drop her into a coma state."

"You're sure it's her who poisoned the tea, though?"

"Close to one hundred percent. Still, someone else could have spiked the drink. Not much chance of it, but possible. Even with Yellow out of it until I bring her back, I'm on my guard."

He listened.

Fear and trembling permeated her speech patterns. As mentally strong a twenty-year-old as he could imagine, she'd come undone.

He listened as she'd related the evening's event in full detail, knowing full well that every word was from the heart. That they'd had history was like saying former American President Ronald Reagan got the Soviets' attention when he forced the dismantling of that empire. Undeniable.

When her breathing, endemic of a severe anxiety attack, abated, Crayle knew what he must do.

"I'll be right there! As soon as I can! We need to keep in touch." He waited. "Ling?"

CHAPTER 3

The president called back. He realized the team needed a break. He gave them orders to a place south of Big Bear that he knew personally. A place of calm.

The Cobra and Hummer, brought there by a special Micmac remote control device, sequenced up the elevator from the quarry hospital, then proceeded north. Crayle knew getting anywhere near the freeways would be worse than stop and go. It would be stop. Any more bombs, and they'd be sitting ducks. He headed them north to the tiny town, Lucerne Valley, then east. Then, south. They blew through Yucca Valley and continued south on every little back road they could find. They achieved their destination two hours later.

Temecula, California sits in a fertile valley about fifty-four miles north of San Diego. The area is known for its touristy Old Town, but far more for its vineyards. Magus and Hekka Crayle pulled into one of the most prominent, Callaway, in their red Cobra. The quarter mile uphill driveway provided an immediate countryside feel as it twisted and turned through the rows of vines, and culminated in a moderate-sized parking lot.

By now, both were quite used to the stares and comments the top scale sports car evinced. A smile back and a "thank you" was the standard, non-engaging response.

The sky set the standard Southern California mood with a few puffy white clouds on a medium blue background. The weather people on TV mentioned 'partly cloudy' so often, it seemed like a recording.

The day affected a perfect mood. Perfect except that it bore a close temporal relationship to the five nuclear device detonations to the northwest that had headed toward Big Bear.

As the two walked the fifty yards to the restaurant, Crayle offered the first observation. "Kimbel … I mean, the president … picked this spot with great care. I like it."

Hekka produced her minimalist Serrano smile. "He picked it because you can see forever across these rolling hills of vines and also observe the only way in or out. There should have been a sign at the bottom: Spies Only."

"Now there's a great idea. A restaurant for spies only. You can't eat or drink anything, and you can't say anything. Other than that … "

"Peaceful."

He entered the doorway and mentioned a reservation under Stones. They were seated directly.

Five minutes later, a fully-optioned Hummer parked beside their car. Its contents poured forth and traipsed over to join the Crayles.

"It didn't take you long. Any trouble finding the place?"

"Not at all," Phoebe said. "Micmac has his new GPS system, and we almost flew here."

Their two travel companions, both pilots, joined in. "As a matter of fact, we could have flown. A lot faster and a lot less bumpy." Jack Sommers ex-wife, Marli, glared at Micmac. Replete in her bright red lipstick and Hollywood sunglasses, she took a seat.

"Good to see you, Marli." Crayle smiled.

"Hmph."

The final guest—Jack's current wife, Flori—took the remaining seat. "Micmac insisted we leave the 7 and 8 at Jack's airport. In fact, he claimed it was on Jack's orders."

She referred to the CIA's Dassault Falcon 7X and 8X maxed-out business jets they utilized for their missions.

Marli folded her arms across her chest. "Another reason for me to have divorced him."

While the rest of the team focused on getting caught up, they scarcely noticed as Micmac pulled a game controller from a small duffel.

A noise emanating from north of their location caught their attention. All heads spun in that direction.

There, coming over the rolling hills, were two business jets. Their wing tips were only separated by about 20 feet.

"Oh, no!" Flori cried out.

Marli sat speechless.

The two aircraft were exact matches for those flown by the women.

Their heads spun back around to catch Micmac toggling the pair of joysticks on the device. "This is why I needed that auto-drive car I had in my front yard. For the technology." He beamed as the two jets screamed over head.

"That's why we couldn't fly here. You planned this, this stunt," Marli accused.

"Look!" Flori exclaimed. "There are two tiny videos split-screened on his phone. He is getting a visual out of the front windows. Micmac, put our rides right back where they belong. Better, land them at the nearest—"

"Already in progress, ladies. I have them on Auto Land. After lunch, I'll drop you off so you can fly them home."

They watched in awe as the jets landed, side-by-side, at the airport.

It took a while for the team members to catch their breath. Flori glanced over at Crayle, breaking the silence.

"And where are Lenny and Alona?"

"Lenny has gotten a bug to relive part of his childhood. His father had taken him to some place in the New Hampshire mountains. He wanted Alona to see it, as well. I called and she said they were on their way there now. We'll catch up with them at a later date."

Phoebe couldn't resist. "My sympathies go out to the Live Free or Die state. They'll have to decide which one he deserves."

That brought some much needed laughter. Phoebe wasn't done.

"If he doesn't get us our babies back, like now, I can tell you which one."

Crayle took back the gavel before the 'on loan' FBI agent could really launch on Lenny. "Look, all of you. The president figured this to be a perfectly safe rendezvous site in light of what just happened west of Big Bear. Given all that's on our plate, he wanted us to collect up and plot our futures."

"With nuclear weapons coming our way, how did he plan we do that?"

"He wants us back in Washington. Actually, Manassas."

"Oh, the old off-the-books underground lair that Jack calls home."

"It's bomb proof. Look, we have to find a way forward that doesn't have these miniaturized nuclear devices in it. We don't know who deployed these recent five, but we do know where they came from. That they were small and emitted no radiation leaves only one possible source."

"Yeah, your Chinese friend. Ling."

"I know her well enough that she wouldn't be down with selling any more of these to the world."

"Magus. With Chin Yao-wu turned to paste by one of those things in the ancient capitol, Xian, she's now the Empress of China. No one can do anything, such as manufacturing nuclear bombs, that she can't stop. Am I right?"

"I've known her for a few years. And especially those first two years when I was over there producing the Blackstone Strategy for Chin."

"So she then marries the adoptive father, who destroyed the communist regime and replaced it with himself. And the bombs kept coming."

"That's right. The three we managed to avoid in Australia's Red Center were purchased after Emperor Chin's death. She was already empress. It's her now."

Crayle knew this conversation would be difficult. His former relationship with the beautiful young Chinese seemed to lurk in the background of his relationship with Hekka. "The bombs and their use as strategic political weapons need to come to an end. That means the manufacturing capability must be terminated."

"With extreme prejudice," Micmac added.

"It's looking like I'll have to go there and..."

"No. Someone else. Have Jack send a team."

"Hekka, it has to be me. She trusts me explicitly and implicitly. Plus, she has intel we need. She knows details about the supply lines, the manufacturing facilities, and the distribution channels."

"That's not all, though. There are still these Illuminé crazies embedded all over the planet. I remember mention of South America from somewhere."

"Kianna from the Australian intel agency mentioned it."

"Maybe that's who set off these most recent bombs."

Their conversations came to a halt. Down Rancho California Road from the west, a train of black hemi Chargers raced their way. Then, over the hills and crashing through the vineyards came a half dozen black SUV's. All headed their way.

"Vehicles! Now!" Crayle cried out.

Since President Stones had reserved the entire restaurant for this occasion, there were no other patrons to panic and impede their exit.

They raced for the Cobra and Hummer. Crayle and Hekka in first, squealed from the lot onto the twisty little driveway. Headed down hill.

Micmac yelled out as they neared the Hummer. "Phoebe! Shotgun!" He indicated her Glock with his hand. He jumped in while she took the front passenger seat. Flori and Marli jumped in behind.

The pair of cars were out of the vineyard before the vehicular onslaught could reach them. But not by much.

Crayle took the lead.

He headed them away.

He headed them east.

Toward Hollywood's home away from home.

Toward Palm Springs.

CHAPTER 4

The road heading east was a four-lane boulevard typically clogged with a lot of traffic. Fortunately, there was a great deal of road work being done and the flagmen at both ends of a two mile section were just switching traffic directions. The space between was temporarily empty.

First a Cobra at full song, then a maxed-out Hummer. They blew by the astonished motorists and workers who had no time to point out the Construction Zone Speed Limit signs, which demanded a maximum speed of fifteen miles per hour. And past them, the other signs threatening double fines for any drivers who exceeded the mandate.

Then the black Hemi Chargers. After them, the black SUV's.

Gunmen in the rear seats of the oncoming Chargers fired at the workmen. Not to kill them, but to explode from their hands the walkie-talkies that could summon the authorities. The hit team's orders were explicit. Take out the targets, or don't come back.

As Crayle pushed the uber sports car to its limit, giving little respite on the corners, Hekka noticed something to their left.

"Look! Animals in steel!"

Sure enough. To that side sat an array of animals, including dinosaurs, made from steel. Apparently some time ago. All bore the characteristic rust color of oxidation.

"We'll have to swing back and pick up a few for the front yard," Crayle responded. "Later."

"How can we think of such trivia in the middle of a fire fight?"

"Abnormal is the new normal."

"I seem to have misplaced our abnormal thinking caps."

"Don't need the caps, Hekka. Call Phoebe. Have her ask Micmac where are those tricked-up planes when we need them?"

The landscape east of Temecula continued the warped flatness they had left behind. To either side grew typical desert foliage, each plant staking out an imaginary claim such that the others maintained about a ten foot distance.

Outgunned and outnumbered, Crayle needed to snatch away the pursuers' advantage.

Hekka called Phoebe via the Cobra's voice-actuated system.

"You want what!" she exclaimed.

"Magus says get it done, Phoebe. It's our only hope."

She turned to her husband, and relayed the message.

"He wants us to swap seats! At eighty miles an hour! With curves!"

She holstered her Glock, then moved her legs over to his side.

"Well?"

"Take the wheel. Slide over the top."

She grabbed the wheel with her left hand and pressed sideways, her head at maximum angle due to the roof.

He wedged under her as they rounded a sharp curve.

Bullets continued to slam the car, but its special construction kept them outside.

Two minutes after beginning the evolution, they'd successfully made the transition. Followed by a great deal of huffing and puffing.

Micmac now had the passenger seat. Phoebe, quite adept with her own Porsche 911, maintained the velocity of the vehicle, corners and all.

Micmac pulled out his modified remote control.

Flori and Marli read his mind. "Oh no you don't!" they chorused.

Both attempted to remove their seat belts and relieve the former SEAL of his new toy. They discovered that the automatic locking mechanism for the car had been enhanced by said former SEAL to lock the seat belts at the same time it locked the doors.

"Put that down!" Marli yelled. "Those aircraft belong to the CIA via a few proprietaries that we're not disposed to reveal!"

Micmac just smiled. To himself.

Shortly, the Crayles ducked, as did the three women in the Hummer as a Falcon 7X and 8X screamed low overhead. Headed west.

The team committing the assault went wide-eyed as the jets came into view. The driver of the lead Charger started for the brakes. The man in charge assessed the situation. "They're just business jets! *Go!*"

Micmac had modified them so that what appeared to be the wind speed measuring pitot tubes had become mini-gun barrels rifled and ready. Much to the chagrin of both Marli and Flori, he'd had the wing fuel tanks minimized to allow for the surfeit of ammunition those weapons required. At 6,000 rounds per minute.

He watched the small high definition screen on the device and managed two joysticks to keep the aircraft separate. As the targets came into view, he pressed the buttons marked ***Go!*** on the left and right.

Mini-guns don't rat-tat-tat, they hum. And they did so now.

This type of ultra weapon fired so much lead so fast, they'd even been used in the Vietnam War to clear paths in the jungle. Or so went the lore.

In this instance, they tore through the just laid asphalt, launching it in all directions as the invading enemy ran right into the onslaught. Surely a number of government regulations had been violated, but

Micmac didn't care a nit. Like Crayle, he had the president on speed dial.

The mini-guns shredded the Chargers and the SUV's. Absolutely. Shredded.

The gunfire sent one black Charger sloshing into a wet asphalt patch. Others exploded, sending flaming Ferals flying.

Twisted around to get a full view of the action, Flori's Brazilian mutated to passable Texan with, "Whew, doggies! Sum bitch!"

"Head 'em home, Micmac," Marli added. "If you can, modify the tail numbers on their high def tail displays when they're out of sight. Send them to Palm Springs."

He smiled. "Changed them before the attack. Changing back …" He pressed two more buttons. "… now!"

Phoebe placed her free hand on her gadget-man husband's thigh and closed the book on the current chapter.

"I do so love you, Micmac!"

• • •

As the team started down Highway 74 toward the Palm Springs expanse, a light snow began to fall. Not daunting to the pursuers even as it intensified.

Hekka, riding shotgun in the Cobra, accessed a tablet computer. "Uh, oh!"

"What?"

"There's been a scramble at MCAS Miramar."

"That's the Marine Corps air base on the north side of San Diego. South of here." Although her brothers were 101st Airborne, Crayle knew she could use an explanation. "Scramble means an emergency rush job for getting several fighter jets up and out. Not good."

"Scramble at March Air Force Base!"

"Northwest of here. We need to get our aircraft down and our cars somewhere out of sight."

CHAPTER 5

Quite finished with the Illuminé mercenaries, the Crayle Cobra and the MacKay Hummer escaped east, away from Temecula, on to Highway 74. The cars blew by the Aguanga Indian Reservation intersection, the village called Anza after a famous California desert region, and finally the giant ice cream cone replica and advertisement alongside the road.

The roadway for the final cruise into Palm Springs wound around and bobbed up and down very similar to Highway 18 from Big Bear Valley down to the CIA's covert quarry hospital. They didn't waste any time, but were especially watchful for the black ice as prevalent on 18 this time of year.

The Crayles and MacKays arrived safely. The pursuers had been not so lucky, attempting to catch a man with racing driver skills and intel operative instincts. And his companion with her own collection of severe abilities. Nor the FBI Agent with her .45 caliber Glock 30. Or her husband, the gadget man, with his ultra gadgets, two remote control business jets with substantial fire power.

Far away on the eastern seaboard, Lenny and Alona received the same exfil directive as the others from Jack Sommers at his Manassas underground headquarters. Their plane made a u-turn prior to reaching their destination. They and the three babies transited the country west in record time.

Upon their arrival at the Palm Springs airport, the Crayles and MacKays quickly retrieved their respective babies. They added the Lipschitz trio to the back seat of Micmac's Hummer, and trekked off for the Desert Springs resort not far away.

The three villas sat side-by-side and each sported a concrete patio facing one of the resorts golf fairways. The late afternoon sun pushed westward to the mountains that bounded the desert valley. Crayle gathered the crew for some wine and cheese and banter. No serious talk. Banter.

"I know we're not supposed to talk about work, but Jack said he wanted us to get a couple days of rest and then meet up back at Manassas. All of us. Babies, too."

Phoebe checked her watch. "Let's see. The No Work rule lasted twenty-seven seconds before being broken by team member Lenny. That's a record."

Crayle intercepted the mayhem about to unfold. "Rule … reset … now! No more work talk. So, Alona, how did you like New Hampshire?"

"Well, if we had actually landed, the train ride up Mount Washington would have been grand. The view of the snow-dusted mountains? Oh!" She paused for effect. "Just fine, Mag."

"How about a rule under which no one speaks. At all. Here, everyone, have some of this fine California wine."

"Did you say whine?"

"No, Lenny. I said wine."

They did manage, after the third glass, to relax into soft talk. No weapons. No battles. No nukes. Soft talk.

"So, Micmac. Any new inventions?" Crayle started it off.

"As a matter of fact. I've thought of one. Nothing fabricated yet. But here's how it would go.

"I've invented an explosive golf ball. I describe them to Lenny in his back yard. The balls are activated via the CIA Universal Remote. There are low-charge ones for testing. They have lower numbers, one through ten, to indicate relative strength. I then tell Lenny not to touch anything. I place one on the ground, not seeing him pick up the remote. There is a small boom. I take off after a fleeing Lenny. I catch him. I am about to give him what for when Alona steps out. *What's going on? What was that noise?* she says. I dust off Lenny. *I was explaining my new invention to your husband when he slipped*, I say."

Lenny appeared puzzled. "How did I slip?"

No one uttered a word.

Not long afterward, they witnessed a beautiful desert sunset, then the MacKays and the Lipschitzes excused themselves and headed to their own rooms. Crayle saw them out and returned to the patio.

• • •

Crayle decided he needed to double source Jack's *Op Crayle* story right after a talk with him, not giving Jack time to warn Hekka. He settled into a chair next to her on the villa's patio.

She knew her husband well. The lack of an up front greeting produced the question, "Something on your mind?"

"That you were there at the Tack Store on my first public outing after the crash, and saved my life, was one major miracle. I have to tell you, there's been a couple of times I've second guessed the whole thing."

"I wondered if it'd gone that way."

"You did?"

"I saw the possibility it could appear like I was the protective squad. Even supplied by Jack himself. No. When I was a little girl, my father would head into that store. I'd stand outside and just stare at that big Bowie knife in the window. I wanted it so bad. My father said I was too young. Later, when I'd grown and happened by the store, there it sat. Still unsold. As if it had waited for me. I had the money, and stepped inside."

"You were old enough to touch it."

"The shop owner knew us well and had watched me ogle it as a child. Watched me devour it with my eyes. Knives were not just an ornament for my Serrano ancestors. They were necessary for life itself. The ten-inch Bowie knife was all that history writ large."

"Then along comes a CIA mind experiment named Magus Crayle."

"One of the many wisdoms I picked up from my father: when push comes to shove, you make the best of it with whatever you have at hand. I followed that wisdom."

"And saved my life."

"Bottom line, I first met Jack after you did. No intrigues here, I'm afraid."

"Damn! Just when you need an intrigue, you come up empty."

• • •

The sun rose on the team's day two in Palm Desert. The adults achieved a sound sleep, which meant the babies slept through the night, as well.

Holding a sleeping baby and having your phone ring—the one that's in your purse on a table ten feet away—can be a challenge. Hekka Crayle was more than used to challenges. She welcomed those that were non-lethal.

"Hello?"

"This is Kianna. Kianna Tarni."

Hekka did not have to struggle with recall. The Australian spy had been inserted high into the Aussie mining magnate, Hamilton Farrell, operation. Right next to the top man himself.

"Thank you once more for saving our lives."

"All in a day's work. Though, the three small nuclear devices posed about as serious a threat as could be imagined. So, how's your baby doing now that you have your own nuclear family?"

"She glows." Hekka caught herself. "I mean, our little Kianna—your namesake—is just fine. She's currently fast asleep. But I'm thinking there's something on your mind. An update?"

"It seems the minds of we indigenous people, no matter how dispersed geographically, connect on the same wavelength."

Her reference to Hekka's Serrano Indian half and her own Aboriginal origins seemed to have a basis in fact.

"We've had time for our federal hazmat people to examine the site at Ulurú. Would you like to hear their assessment?"

"I've got peace and quiet at least for now. Fill me in."

"Here goes. The three directional bombs you and your team reversed in direction blew their entire energy down each of those horizontal mining tunnels. Since the tunnels terminated at Farrell's three mines, the force wiped out the mines and the remainder of the force vented upward into the sky. Had they not been reversed, they would have blown the sacred Ulurú rock into dust. The prevailing winds would've covered Australia with a thick red cloud."

"And the indigenous would have revolted. Others, too."

"Ham would have become the next Aussie president."

"His goal all along."

"He'd removed the mine workers under the guise of a holiday of sorts. They are all safe. The visitor center above the hub of the tunnels survived, believe it or not."

"What of Farrell's guests, the Lalumière daughters? And him, Lalumière? And Pattie?"

"No idea. Anyone still in the vicinity of the mines above ground, or caught in the tunnels, would have been vaporized. Not even DNA could've survived."

"I do so hope they are gone forever. But, you and Farrell escaped. Those others weren't with you?"

"As you remember, while the count down was still underway, we all drove back to the three mines two-by-two. Ham and I reached the diamond mine. He had an escape craft, a little two-person vertical take off, and we were out of there. We escaped to the east coast. That's where he left me and got the submersible he used to attack Magus."

"I'm declaring the whole thing over."

"Oh, I left out a part. The explosions collapsed the tunnels. Ulurú itself suffered not even a scratch. You might let Magus know. Our honor wall at the Australian Intelligence Service now has an additional six stars for you and your team. We owe you a great deal."

"As you said, all in a day's work."

"One last thing. In New Zealand, they're still trying to identify the diminutive individual who zip-lined onto the soccer pitch at Eden Stadium, grabbed the fourth of Ham's bombs, and saved the day along with beaucoup Aussie and Kiwi lives."

"You're telling me Lenny's a national hero? You know, he does that sort of thing when not being a genuine pain in the ass. Meaning infrequently."

"The Kiwis don't care. If he ever returns, he's getting a hero's welcome."

"Oh, there's baby Kianna now. Have to go. We'll talk again."

"Yes, we will."

• • •

The next day, the team was off again. Flori and Marli flew the 7X and 8X hands on. They headed toward the Washington, D.C. area. Under President Stones orders.

CHAPTER 6

Jean-Marc Lalumière, son of Sylvain, stood fully naked as he spoke into his Smartphone. In true French fashion, he waved his free hand for emphasis as if he were sorry he couldn't wave both. He knew he could put the caller on speaker, but not in this situation. Not when the other individual was of his own ultra secret society, Illuminé.

The Swedish queen, also unencumbered by clothing and still lying on their tryst bed, had not yet received the initiation necessary to bring her in as a major player in the organization. And she might not live long enough to achieve that pinnacle.

Frustrated, she couldn't understand a word of what Jean-Marc was saying. Somewhere along the line, he'd learned a language she recognized as Swiss-German that her paramour used for secrecy. She'd heard of the American Wind Talkers of World War II, whose Navajo language possessed a similar inscrutable nature.

He finished. Disgusted, he tossed the phone onto the royal vanity, and stood facing her, hands on hips.

"That went well," observed the queen.

Light-hearted repartee was excluded from his universe at times like this. "There was an attack on the Crayle team today. Five nuclear devices. Which they survived."

"If the three tried in Australia didn't produce the desired result on them, what made anyone think two more would produce different results. This team of six seems indestructible. Other-worldly protected. And what's next? Ten?"

"That's not all. They escaped to some place in Southern California called Temecula. Our surveillance located them there. A large hit team went after them. Ferals."

"They failed, too?"

"They're the toughest that the German race could produce. Real blonde hair. Spiked. Tips colored for team recognition. The Crayle bunch apparently ate them for lunch."

"That German heavy paramilitary units get wiped out is good for Sweden. We've experienced the Aryan supremacists before. Not good."

"I get the point," Jean-Marc noted. "My France bore the brunt of their fury more than once."

"So we both win. Look, I know this is difficult for you. But with the most certain demise of your father, Sylvain, and that Pattie woman he kept, we must now move forward. The French people still clamor for the legendary Man In The Iron Mask character your father portrayed under the acronymic moniker, Mitim. He was the rightful heir to the monarchy re-established at the Roman Colosseum by the pope and the Monaco prince, as you've related to me. You were there."

"I . . . we must organize this coup d'état facilitated by the exile of the former French leaders, who met their nuclear demise in China."

"I'll call the pope. He can perform the coronation."

"Coronation?"

"You are the same six-foot-six as your father. No one actually saw his face. You just need to put on the mask, *et voilá*!"

"We will have to decide on the timing. The when."

"And *when* do we announce my additional role as Queen of France? My French is quite good, you know."

"It appears that French and sex are synonyms, then."

She smiled. "Come back to bed."

He started toward her, then stopped. "What about the danger posed by the Russians?"

"The czarina who's become Vladimir's other half? On their path to re-instituting the Russian monarchy?"

"I'm not ready for surprises from them."

"I'm not worried a bit. I've been saving a surprise for you."

He said nothing, but knew each of them still held secrets. He knew he was in for a shock. "The czarina?"

The Queen of Sweden waited a beat.

"She's my cousin."

CHAPTER 7

The Russian president exhibited a particularly foul mood on this cold Moscow morning. His adjutant, a descendant of the eponymous and infamous mad monk, Rasputin, of czarist times, knew when to be a good listener.

The calendar pushed further into the Fall season. The cold became a biting cold whenever the winds blew into Moscow, and it seemed they always did. The leader of the Russian Federation and his number one lieutenant sat comfortably before a large fireplace nursing hot toddies, the third for each.

"What is your read on the state of the current situation, my friend?"

Raspi glanced at the president with one raised eyebrow. "I speak freely?"

"Of course."

"We have entered a blah phase."

"Blah?"

"An American term. No excitement. Nothing to motivate the people in a positive manner."

President Vladimir considered the response.

"Perhaps you are right. But, another topic. I'm dead serious about Alaska. I studied this while in the KGB. Russia was robbed. And when the capitalist spies reported we were taking renewed interest, they trained Alaskans in both espionage and resistance. The most hardy of that lot. Stay-behind operatives, they were called. Operation STAGE was the code name. That's what they called it."

"CIA?"

"No. The CIA, by law, cannot operate in the United States. Instead, FBI. Intense training in nuclear, biological, and chemical warfare. NBC. Recognizing ships and aircraft, and coded communication. The DIANA Cryptosystem, it was called. And a whole host of techniques. Evading detection. Hand-to-hand combat. The list goes on and on. Regular citizens trained as operatives. Natives of the environment. They didn't stand out at all."

"You sound jealous."

He nodded. "We never invaded. Our program stood down in the early 1950's."

"What now?"

"There are a couple of options. We can stage a full conventional assault, and face off against the world's best fighter squadrons, or just wipe the oil reserves with these small nuclear devices the Chinese have. Minus the radiation sponges."

"What? Irradiate the Alaska oil supplies in order to raise yours in value? And the United States would not deem that an act of war? At the nuclear level?"

"We must make the destruction appear as an American program gone wrong. A mistake."

"Or somehow blame the Chinese, whose fingerprints are all over these types of bombs."

"You have something, Raspi. Perhaps the North Koreans, who could have gotten them from China. Easily. Think about it. Would

Beijing's power brokers allow Pyongyang to have its own nuclear weapons? Or would they sneak in the devices? Then, explode them to give the Americans fits?"

"If the rest of the world blames either or both of those countries, we win. All you need then is an NK motive. Not hard to imagine."

"All I need is someone who connects to the Chinese empress and to the American president."

"All you need is a willing American spy, Magus Crayle."

"Yes. If I cannot have Alaska peacefully, I may need to send the nukes there."

"You would destroy it?"

"I would create an alternate reality—at 8,000 degrees Fahrenheit."

"You are making me hungry."

"How's that?"

"Baked Alaska?"

Uncharacteristic, the president laughed out loud. His adjutant began to feel a warmth from the man. But not a time to change from the previous somber mood.

"Please tell me more, Vladimir, why the American state is so critical."

The president grimaced. "Raspi, I cannot continue to pose for photo opportunities, shirtless astride horses, or holding sporting rifles and expect the Russian people to elevate me to the god-like status I deserve. Don't you see? If I pry that state, America's largest, from their grasp, I'll have it. I will become czar. Not president. Czar!"

The aide had heard this before. Russian diplomats had already approached the United States president, Stones, regarding a repurchase. The man had made himself clear. In the negative. Best to push an alternative. "The czarina, a true and verified Romanov, is ready for her own destiny. The people will accept that. And they will accept you as her mate." He paused for effect. "Czarina. Czar. A royal solution to our country's problems."

"I do believe the czarina is putting on some weight. Did you notice, Raspi?"

"I think you are noticing because you permit her to be on top. She is exceptionally ambitious, Vladimir. Bad idea. You may want to reposition."

"You are always grounded and rational, my friend. It's why I don't have you executed." He took a few seconds. "I am kidding, of course."

Raspi had been close to Vladimir for years. Time for a change of subject. "The czarina is in the other room being fitted for her finery. For the day the two of you achieve total control. And establish your bloodline as sacred."

Vladimir, the tough as nails former KGB operative, felt a tingle inside.

His adjutant started away. For a breather. But noticed his boss had something more. Better to remain. And listen.

"Oh, yes, before you go. I almost forgot. We just received a request from that ultra-secret society."

"Didn't they disappear with all that nuclear action not long ago in Australia? And Monte Carlo?"

"The Illuminé lost their top dog down under plus that secret society's head man, respectively. But if the Illuminé still has operatives, they could be an ally going forward."

"Claiming operatives in governments worldwide, we run the risk of some inside your own government. We need time to weed them out. Best you consider a meeting."

"And then I have the Swedish Queen to deal with. And the Aryans—wherever they are—wanting a Fourth Reich. Tell me, Raspi, why I want to head this country."

"Well, you have spirited quite an amount of wealth to safe havens. There's enough to live somewhere warm. Stress free. Safe. Rich."

"As good as that sounds, it doesn't work for me. Leadership is in my blood. I realized during my KGB service that control, total control, is not an option. It is a necessity."

At that point, the czarina paraded through a connecting doorway, stopped, and twirled in her Eighteenth Century regalia. She read the two mesmerized gazes. "Talking politics?"

Vladimir stepped to her and embraced her shoulders. "You look beyond fantastic."

That he'd sidestepped her question spoke volumes. She hadn't gotten as far as she did by ignoring signs, however subtle. This one lacked subtlety. "What's going on?"

CHAPTER 8

Fall weather in Hong Kong. Rain began in the early hours and continued unabated into mid-morning. As it brought life to the abundance of flora and fauna on the island, it brought a gloomy attitude to the people, even in the palace atop Mount Victoria.

Ling An-yee, the young empress of the new Imperial China, watched the downpour as if it would somehow reveal answers to her many questions. Slowly, she backed away from the window. No, she concluded. And she, barely in her twenties, did not possess the necessary life experiences. The much needed answers could only come from one source.

"You're thinking of him again, aren't you?" The voice from behind didn't startle her. She'd known it since her first days at the orphanage.

"You forgot to knock again."

"Knock on what? I came through the floor to ceiling drapes as I always do."

"It's alright. We're sisters."

"Any time you want a little help running your empire, just let me know. It's what sisters are for."

"I appreciate the light-hearted banter. I'm just standing here and watching the city. And pondering what got us to this point. This pinnacle."

"I believe Confucius said, 'beware of pinnacles.'"

"Remember how we studied the past. How, in 1949, Mao Tse-dung created the communist state. And promised a worker's paradise."

"We have that now. I suppose he was true to his word, with a little help from the West. Understand that our 1.4 billion people are confined to a space covering just 3.7 million square miles. Twenty-two provinces. Five autonomous regions. Four cities—Beijing, Tianjin, Shanghai, and Chongqing—under direct, central control. And finally with Hong Kong and Macau as Special Administrative Regions, each demanding democracy. The communist concluded there is no way to govern with other than an iron, unsympathetic fist."

"The lack of prosperity inherent in Mao's ideology led the subsequent leaders to their own pinnacle. Above a precipice. Having no choice, they brought in capitalism in order to pay the bills."

"And fend off an impending revolt by the people."

"Their gamble worked. In came the land of opportunity, and the communists were able to keep total control."

"And their heads."

"True enough, Yellow. The move allowed enterprising Chinese like our adoptive Father, Chin Yao-wu, to enrich themselves in the new stock markets. Just add into the mix the mini-nukes and their potential to reconstruct the geopolitical landscape."

"You always find the political aspects fascinating. You are perfect for your role as empress."

"Are you blowing smoke?"

The question puzzled Yellow. "I don't know that idiom."

"It means are you talking BS."

"Now BS I understand. Here, Empress Ling. Your tea is cold. I'll make a fresh batch."

Yellow took the cup and saucer and headed off.

Almost colliding, another of Chin's daughters passed her through the drapes. She crossed the room to Ling.

"It's getting close, White. A new baby."

"It is the future emperor. I must help you make China ready for him. To ease his burden." She read the concern on Ling's face. "I happened to hear Yellow's assessment that you are thinking of Mr. Crayle again. I can tell. You are."

Ling walked to an original Ch'in period desk and pulled back the chair. Grasping the handles of the drawers on either side, she pulled. She took care to pull them simultaneously and at the same rate. After just four inches, they became immobile.

Next, the two heard a clunk. The center drawer opened. They saw that the noise they'd heard was a cover over the drawer's contents sliding into place. The drawer rotated up, revealing a large tablet computer. Ling retrieved the chair and took a seat.

"I'm going to disable the security sound surveillance, White. I'm also going to enable the floor sensors."

White deduced that she was being brought into Ling's confidence. But why? Why now?

"In this configuration, no one can listen to our conversation. I've decided to bring you up to speed on the things I use in my empress role. You, having the imperial color white, will succeed me if I die before your child can become emperor of China."

This was a little much for the other young woman. Barely in her twenties, she could in an instant become Empress of China, and all that entailed. She made a silent vow to protect Ling at all costs. "You honor me with your confidence."

"You are worthy. And now I shall share information of the greatest import. Just a few years ago, Father Chin became a member of an international and very secret society. In so doing, he agreed to partner with similar successful individuals across the globe. The top echelon of this group decided that the communist regime in China had to go. The group had determined that only monarchs should rule. They believed themselves to be the enlightened—hence their French name, Illuminé—and it was they who should make all decisions for their countries, and rule with an iron fist."

"How is that different from the communists?"

"They saw them as only having seized physical power over the people, but that they were hardly enlightened. Had they been otherwise, they wouldn't have needed to add capital investment and markets in order to pay for their abundant social programs, They would have forecast the need, and already have it."

"Please. Continue."

"Chin brought in a man named Magus Crayle, whom you have met. He was a master strategist, but not of the Illuminé. He developed a strategy for Chin that would result in his displacing the communist government, and reinstituting the imperial rule of his forebear, Ch'in Xihuangdi."

"The creator of China. Long ago."

"2,240 years ago, to be more precise. I... we need Mr. Crayle right now. I hear that the former government leaders, whom I trusted out of convenience and my youth to run the country, are scheming to take my place. I should have known that they would repay me with treachery."

"After the nuclear device detonated in Beijing's Underground City and Chin took power, he imprisoned them on the southern island of Hainan."

"Yes. To make terra cotta warriors for Chin's burial mound."

"What can we do, Empress?"

"We can utilize Mr. Crayle's Blackstone Strategy tactic. We must identify those who are being seditious, herd them into a remote place, and then wipe them out."

"This is a lot for two twenty-year-olds."

"That's why I need Magus. I mean, Mr. Crayle." She noted the Freudian slip, and decided to give White the necessary backdrop she'd kept to herself. "He was here for two years. I was just sixteen when he came."

"Came?"

"Arrived."

"Oh."

"I developed what the Americans call a crush on him. I liked him. One evening after dinner, he escorted me to my room."

"Uh, oh."

Ling smiled as she remembered the moment in full detail. "He's tall. But I went to my tiptoes and kissed him on the lips."

White daughter did a first-class impression of being horrified. "You didn't."

"I did. And I would have done the rest if he'd wanted."

"Father expressly forbade 'the rest' if that's what you're talking about. And he didn't want? Father taught us that all men want."

"He wanted, all right. I could tell. But he was a perfect gentleman about the whole thing. He told me good night, turned on his heel, and left."

"What was Father's problem with sex? Was it just our age?"

"I remember Father's many admonitions on the subject of sex. No, not just our age. It seems his own mother had been defiled by a communist regional official. The man impregnated her... with Father. Recently, I learned he took the ultimate revenge when he found out."

"Well, let's hope that Magus returns your call." White slapped a hand over her mouth.

"It's okay. You can use his given name when we are alone and the multitudes of hidden microphones are disengaged. I with my title and you with Chin's baby are in this together."

They shared a high five. Ling re-engaged security. She stared at her Imperial Smartphone. "Come on, Magus. Call me."

CHAPTER 9

It was Jack Sommers who'd put out the call. All members of the Strategic Solutions Office Crayle team to collect ASAP into the Manassas underground headquarters. Crisis topic: the continued manufacture and distribution of miniaturized nuclear bombs by Chinese empress, Ling An-yee.

Within two hours of the call, the team departed the Palm Springs airport in California, arriving at Virginia's Dulles Airport four hours later. Quickly through a placebo version of security, they boarded the usual caravan of black SUVs and headed to the Manassas battlefield park site. Once they'd paid their entry fees and stepped through the visitor center, they trooped straight to the walled-off set of porta potties and entered the one they knew well. The one that always indicated ***OCCUPIED***.

It was a bit of a squeeze for the six of them. Especially carrying three babies. For a moment, they turned away from each other to pluck the short and curlies necessary for identification. They tossed them into the urinal basin provided, trying hard not to start a giggling match.

In succession, hands were alternately placed on what appeared to be a shiny stainless steel mirror for corroboration by palm print.

Done, the innards of the potty proceeded directly down at the usual express clip. They exited the covert elevator deep underground.

Before they could exit, Lenny turned to Micmac.

"I'm glad they got the smell down. Whew!"

"Give S & T their creds. It did smell authentic."

That the CIA's Science and Technology directorate could provide just about anything for just about any purpose was not lost on them. It had saved their lives with various gadgets several times in the past.

Every member of the team knew one thing. They needed serious down time. Impromptu trips all over the world at breakneck speed, a seeming endless supply of deadly enemies, and the weapon of the future that existed today—the miniature nuclear device—saw them tempting fate on a daily basis.

Jack Sommers race-walked the chartreuse corridor and rounded the last corner in a hurry. With his special Science and Technology variable-darkness sunglasses on six of ten, he was able to withstand the brightness of the hideous wall paint left behind by his predecessor. Beside being a mole for the Illuminé, his former and dearly departed boss, Neil Wohlford, should have stayed away from design cues like wall colors.

With his mind distracted, he pecked the keypad before recalling that he had a proximity pass for that purpose. He extracted it from his RFID protected envelope and quickly entered his office. He utilized a wall-mounted rheostat to ramp up the lighting.

To his right, there they were. The Crayles, MacKays, and Lipschitzes arrayed on Jack Sommers' own sleeper sofa. To his left, he spied an opaque sheet propped up on all sides by Wohlford's French antique armchairs.

"I don't suppose I should ask how you got into my totally secure workspace... being spies and all."

No response. They'd come at his bidding. It was his turn.

Before he could begin on them, Jack couldn't permit something out of place to remain that way. He stepped over to the impromptu tent, and came to an abrupt halt.

"My office," he said. Annoyed, he grabbed a handful of cloth, and yanked it away.

The babies in the three covered bassinettes took the glare of the office's overhead lighting directly and, in no uncertain terms, expressed their displeasure.

With the din of three squalling infants disapproval, he at once realized the sheet's purpose. "You brought the kids!"

"It gets worse," Phoebe advised.

Then, Alona. "We fully understand that this op you cited in getting us here must happen and that we're the only ones for the job."

"Before I get into the details of why I asked you here, give me a sitrep of the recent West Coast action."

Crayle took the lead in apprizing him of every detail of their recent encounters at Big Bear and at the vineyard. None of it surprised Jack. The level of frustration with success after success and no end in sight worried him. When operatives got this amped up, they tended to make mistakes. Fatal mistakes.

"Forget any op my communication may have intimated. Here's what's going to happen. I'm giving you all some down time. One, you deserve it. Two, you'll be eating your own guns if I don't. I'll get right to it. Lenny and Alona. You're off to New Hampshire. You've mentioned it before, so I booked you at the Bretton Arms Inn. You can kick around there looking for Winston Churchill's ghost or whatever. I highly recommend Mount Washington, a short drive away."

Uncharacteristically silent up to the moment, Lenny piped up. "Sounds like a great trip at your expense. Bet I can find a captive audience there for some of my best jokes."

"If you get yourself in any trouble with aforementioned sense of humor, Lipschitz, the department will disavow any knowledge of your existence. Understood?"

"Jeez-Louise. I was kidding."

Jack turned to the MacKays.

"Phoebe. You and guitar man, Micmac, are off to Nashville." He glanced at the former SEAL. "I know you've written some songs. Maybe you can start a third career at the Opry."

"SEAL, spy, singer. Works for me."

"Nicely done. Alliteration and sibilance times three."

The sailor bowed. "Hanging around with Mag."

"Yeah. Here's the deal. Phoebe and Micmac have the Falcon 7X and will drop off Lenny and Alona at the Portsmouth, New Hampshire airport. The Lipschitzes then grab a rental that's been pre-arranged, and, after checking out that coastal town, it's a nice drive to the resort up in the mountains. Then, the MacKays continue on with the jet to Nashville. Oh, I almost forgot. Phoebe, your old boss wants you to drop into Louisville, Kentucky, just north of your destination, and do a little job there. Nothing to shake a stick at, but he told me that you're the only one with the necessary background that's available. As long a time as we've had you on loan from the Bureau, I said okay."

Micmac gave him a look. "How about we fly to Louisville after dropping off Lenny and Alona. We'll get Phoebe installed in an expensive hotel on your card, then I'll make it down to Music City while she's doing this minor gig. We'll keep the 7X with us so I can pick her up when she's finished."

"That leaves you to baby sit," Hekka completed the thought.

Jack's other monumental problems faded into oblivion. He glanced over at the three infants. "No! No! No!"

Micmac responded. "That's the deal, Jack. We're not leaving them anywhere else."

Then, Hekka. "Under each bassinette you will discover a supply of appropriately sized Huggies."

And Phoebe. "We took the liberty of emptying your wine cooler."

Jack spun. "Why's that?"

"The ladies pumped for the entire flight here. It's in there." Crayle provided his best inquisitive expression. "The milk?"

Jack's mind elevated his eyebrows to maximum height in order to express itself.

"You better hope we get back before you run out," Hekka said.

"Jeez-Louise!" Lenny piped in. "Aren't you gonna thank us?"

Jack tried unsuccessfully to proceed. "This is one option. Is suicide the other? I don't want to rush to judgment."

The team members folded their arms.

"It's a deal then. The three babies stay here with me. Or you'll be needing time off from the time off." Jack punctuated the statement with a stare. "Mag and Hekka. Stay behind for a minute." He glared at the others. "Well, what are you waiting for? Rock and Roll!"

The four left.

"And us?"

"If you will, Hekka, I'd like you to stay here with the babies until Flori or Marli returns."

"And Magus?"

"I need him to make a quick sojourn to the wonderful state of Washington. To interview someone for me. He should be back in a couple of days. Once he's back, I've a spectacular trip planned for you both. I'm keeping it a secret for now, but no bombs, bullets, or bad guys. I promise."

"I'd love to spend time with the babies. Magus, go ahead. Rock and Roll!"

An aide showed Hekka and the babies to another room while Jack filled in his master spy on the mission to a very special place near Richland, Washington.

"The others have the Falcon 7X tied up. That leaves your 8X. If you really want me out west." The super spy waited a couple of beats. "What's it going to be, Jack?"

"Wait. Can't you just high tail it out of here and catch up with the others? You know. The tricked out Dassault Falcon 7X?"

Crayle answered. "It's staying with them. Remember? Might as well be in the shop. Gotta be the 8."

"All right. All right. I'll make the call."

"Perfect. And, Jack? Be sure you perform your half of the duties … with the babies?"

His boss grimaced.

"Who knows? *Da-Da* might be their first words."

Jack reddened.

"Out! Out! Out!."

With the team having filed from Jack's office and the babies under Hekka's care in another room, he had a moment of peace. Two quick trips to the airport and they'd be off. Beginning what they believed to be nothing other than a much-needed R & R. Rest and relaxation. Embarking, perhaps, on their most dangerous operation ever.

CHAPTER 10

Phoebe MacKay had been ordered to Louisville, Kentucky for an FBI op. She'd been detailed to the CIA for over two years now, and, to stay in good stead with her boss's boss, she couldn't say no. Her husband Mick, known as Micmac to friends and co-workers, went along for the ride.

They'd been in the air just a couple of hours after leaving the Portsmouth, New Hampshire area. The parting words they'd heard from the Lipschitzes was a Lenny "Whine!" It seemed he thought he should keep the jet and the MacKays could find another way west.

The PA system on the 7X had been its usual quiescent. Until now. "On approach to Louisville International Airport. Buckle up."

Passengers Phoebe and Micmac wondered whether anyone other than pilot Flori could make those few words sound so sexy.

"Check it out, Phoebe. It's beautiful down there."

"Where Kentucky meets Indiana. Separated by the Ohio River. Nice."

"They do horse racing in Kentucky, I believe. Add Indiana and Ohio. Isn't that a trifecta?"

Saved by the bell. Her Smartphone rang. "Special ring. My boss."

She went into the bedroom aft to take the call. With the door closed, she pressed keys to turn the device into an FBI traffic only device. That action separated it from the Company traffic, and vice versa. Another choice provided local, county, or state police communications. The source of these special devices, the Science and Technology directorate, guaranteed that there would be absolutely no crosstalk between any of the three incarnations.

"Howdy, Bransfield," came her boss's Texas charm. "I meant MacKay. Got to bump you up to *my* boss for the *read in*. Neither I nor anyone else will be listening to what is said. His orders."

She heard a few beeps, then the man. She'd not worked with him before.

"Agent MacKay. I'm going to read you in on the Louisville operation. Don't make anything of me jumping in, your boss is in the middle of something. Just make sure there's no one in the room."

Phoebe could tell by the voice that he was antsy about something. She responded.

"My phone provides separation and isolation, but it would be okay for the Company to listen in on this, but they wouldn't be interested. They're not allowed to operate within the United States borders."

"You're right. That would only matter if your surveillance target, a man named Maximillian Gibbs, had connections outside the country. Even then, they'd have to get a FISA warrant. And you know how difficult that is."

Phoebe let that one slide.

The plane landed so smoothly, she didn't fall from her standing position or lose her focus.

"Get yourself settled into the hotel that I prescribed. Take it easy a bit. I'll notify you when it's time to get going on this. It is sensitive, so you'll have to go dark on this one. I'm sure your spouse travelling with you can find something to do in the Upper South."

He proceeded with some operational details. Her questions were few and easily answered. But he knew she was smart. That was what bothered him.

It seemed easy compared to her CIA work over the past two years. Locate the target, watch him, report in. She needed a break and this operation should check a couple of boxes at her employer, the FBI. Then, she'd be back where she felt at home. On the Crayle team. And, if there was a problem with that, her trump card was President Stones. So there.

In short order, the jet taxied to a stop, they loaded their gear into a waiting yellow SUV, and headed to the river side Galt House Hotel and Suites.

• • •

The Conservatory at The Galt Hotel in Louisville was like a glass panel tube running from one building, east across Fourth Street, to the second building. Main Street bounded it on the south side, the Ohio River on the north.

Phoebe entered from the west side. She sent an encrypted message to Micmac to let him know her location.

He received it a short distance away at the river's edge, where he checked out a docked paddle wheeler. His curiosity sated, he headed up to the hotel. As he entered the Conservatory area past a pizza bar's order window, he spotted his wife in a chair by the bar.

Seeing him, she stood and extended her hand. "You must be Colonel Mustard."

He laughed. It felt good. "What? In the Conservatory with a … um … what's my weapon?"

"You know damn well what your weapon is."

"Oh, yeah. The Babies R Us thing."

"Hmmm. Look, this op could take a week. Why not take the opportunity, and scoot on down to Nashville like we discussed. We can meet up in some place like Memphis. Right after you strut your country side at the Grand Ole Opry."

"Sure. I've heard they are down to just 20,000 singer-songwriters in Music City."

"None like you. Blend Rock and Country. Start a trend."

"Hard to start a trend that began fifty years ago."

"You'll find a way. A guy that found a way to create our beautiful daughter."

"I just loosened the lid."

"How about loosening it once more before you head off to Nashville?"

"I should stay here with you. 'Til this FBI op is over."

"I'll be fine. Boss says it's just a little thing to keep my hand in at the Bureau. No big deal. He promised me. Still, I have to go dark. How's about you make your way down to Nashville and show 'em what you got."

"Sounds good." He stood, giving her a hand up. "About that lid…"

They took the elevator and walked, hand-in-hand, to their room, and were nearly naked before their door closed. Micmac was in the rental car headed south to Nashville four hours later.

CHAPTER 11

As she rubbed the sleep from her eyes the next morning, Phoebe realized the stark contrast between FBI and CIA work. The FBI had to obey all laws of the United States or any other country in which it operated. They were about law and order 100%. In contrast, the Company—Mag Crayle One and Mag Crayle Two's world—was about pushing the American agenda around the world, whatever it took. Break foreign laws, turn foreign citizens into traitors, but absolutely no operations within America's borders or its territories. Against the law. Very against the law.

She rode the elevator down to the second floor Café Magnolia for breakfast. A fried pickle appetizer, Double Stacked Mag Burger as a tribute to her friend and colleague, and a caramel-soaked Derby Pie. Then, back to the room.

While she waited for the call to start the surveillance op, she decided to check out Louisville. Gather some souvenirs while the down time lasted.

She checked her city layout app, then walked the several blocks to Louisville's visitor center, picked up recommendations, and purchase two Louisville—how to pronounce it—T-shirts. Of the several choices, she preferred *Lou-uh-vull.* Never *Lou-us-vil,* the clerk admonished. The southern accent would have to come next.

As she walked to the sights, she knew one thing. She missed him. She called him the Big Lug and other things, but she was in love. One thing stood in the forefront of her mind. Back with Micmac to Manassas and their baby ASAP.

• • •

Phoebe had a day to kill. She toured out to the world famous Churchill Downs race track and bought two more T-shirts. Then, back to downtown and a tour of the Louisville Slugger baseball bat factory on Main Street.

"Could you make one up for me. For someone special," she'd asked.

"Certainly can," the young man answered. "Here's the list."

She checked it out. "That was easy." She gave him her choice and watched while it was fabricated from a solid oak blank. A Willie Mays Special she'd give him. While he admired it, she'd stand behind him and remove her clothes. He'd hear her whisper, "Hey, Sailor" or something to that effect, and turn around.

"Well, put the bat down, my dear. I think you're about to score."

• • •

Packaged custom-made bat in hand, she took a tour of the nearby Evan Williams Kentucky Bourbon distillery on the way back to the hotel. One bottle should be plenty, she reasoned. Worn out, she trekked the couple of blocks to the Galt House Hotel and her room, and plopped down on the bed. Before dozing off, there was but one thought on her mind.

She missed him.

• • •

Phoebe woke the next day. She hoped to get the call, wrap things up, and be with Micmac as soon as possible. She realized that running with the Crayle CIA team for the past couple of years may have slowed her a half step or so in FBI work, but she had the confidence and the chops to get things done. She recalled the *read in* delivered by her boss's boss.

He'd added that this should just be a few day gig when it started in earnest. And that the ***Go*** signal would be the next time she heard from him.

Fine. Off to spend the morning at the nearby Muhammad Ali Center. When her father had been stationed at military bases, Phoebe had taken up boxing. That was a fact Lenny Lipschitz had learned the hard way, when they first met.

She'd pay her respects at the Center, then await the call.

CHAPTER 12

The CIA's *Reservations By Darryl* placed Micmac in a Nashville corporate apartment on Church Street. Just in time for lunch and with a full, but un-stocked kitchen, he slipped across the street to Puckett's Grocery and Restaurant. The menu-specified *down home cookin'* lived up to its billing. A few guitar props on the walls had him feeling right at home. And there was a band stand. Music City, indeed.

He worried about leaving Phoebe to fend for herself. Then, he realized how foolish he was being. FBI operatives always seemed to have backup somewhere nearby. And, if someone could handle just about anything, it would be her.

Micmac had so many things to do and see. He needed to move fast. To be efficient. Phoebe could call at any time. He checked the list.

Gibson solid body guitar factory.

No, he had one of those and would be tempted to buy five or six more. Better skip that one.

Margaritaville.

Done. He made the visit, checked his watch to see if it was five o'clock yet, and quaffed two of the special margaritas anyway.

Next on to Legends with its outdoor mural of some very famous country stars. Another couple of drinks, and he decided to take a breather. Work off some of the alcohol. He walked back to the apartment, and took a snooze.

Two hours later, his eyes popped open.

Micmac checked his special ops watch. Ah, time for the last item on his list.

In short order, he put on a ***Cryin' Dyin' or Goin' Someplace*** shirt he took with him everywhere, hopped in the rental car, and headed to the Grand Ole Opry. There, he jumped a tour group and found himself standing on the famous stage. He stepped up to a microphone. "Oh, for a Les Paul guitar and a Marshall amp," he spoke into it. "If only Phoebe could see me now."

The notion faded. She couldn't see him now. He took a selfie. When comms were no longer black, he'd share it with her. He shook his head. His next thought: he needed to get back to Louisville. Another head shake. No. Phoebe had this. He'd head off to Memphis to set things up there. A good reunion when she flew in on the 7X. And some serious lid loosening. He popped back into the present, and glanced around.

The tour guide seemed to be checking him over.

She was cute.

He was married.

"Former military?"

He nodded.

"Stop by tonight. We're having our annual military appreciation night."

Now, there was good luck. An annual event and he, by pure circumstance, was there. He nodded.

"Name?"

"Mick MacKay. Friends call me Micmac."

"Ooh. Micmac. I like that."

He glanced down to his left.

She saw the ring. "Oops."

He took the ticket for the evening show, thanked her, and departed back to the apartment.

On the drive back, he still couldn't get Phoebe out of his head. They'd never been apart this long. He decided to ramp up the number of things he could share with her when they were together again.

He added such an item that night. At the Opry concert, he was called up on stage by the same tour guide from before. Then came the grand surprise. She handed him a Gibson Les Paul that happened to be plugged into a Marshall amplifier. "You're on."

He responded. "If Phoebe could only see me now."

There he was. Standing on the stage at the world-famous Grand Ole Opry with a collection of musicians known by everyone on the planet. He thought his smile was so big, it might crack his face.

They played a country rock tune that everybody knew. He bowed, and headed for his back-of-the-auditorium, view everything and everybody seat. Best in the house.

• • •

The next morning, Micmac packed up and started west, but quickly modified his route. He turned south toward Lynchburg, Tennessee.

A couple of hours later, he arrived in the town square.

It seemed that everything there had some manner of Jack Daniels motif. He wondered if the town had a patron saint named Saint Jack.

No. He thought of their boss, Jack Sommers. There probably wasn't a saint by that name.

He purchased a case of Tennessee Honey and a couple of boxes of whiskey-infused cakes at the Jack Daniels store.

There. Enough for now, and for when he reunited with Phoebe.

He filled up with gas, and headed to Memphis.

CHAPTER 13

Before the second day concluded, Mick MacKay, known to friends and colleagues as Micmac, drove his rental car into Memphis from the east. No one needed to know about the slight detour south from Nashville to the Tennessee whiskey holy ground in Lynchburg, Jack Daniels distillery.

He turned onto Lieutenant George W. Lee Avenue and arrived at the Westin Memphis Beale Street hotel. He'd reserved it with a thirty second call to the team's Nova Scotia covert travel specialist during his stop at Lynchburg. He'd also made a list of attractions that were, for him, a must see.

Graceland. The Elvis Nirvana.

Peabody Hotel, and its famous ducks.

Sun Studio. The place that recorded Elvis.

Blues Hall of Fame. Enough said.

Rock 'n' Soul Museum. Same.

Beale Street. Memphis music central.

Hard Rock Café. T-shirts for him and Phoebe. And the giant burger.

Blues City Café. Gumbo so addictive, it should be listed by the DEA.

Paddleboat ride. On the Mississippi River.

And he probably only had one day for all of it.

Micmac's custom GPS guided him to the hotel. He intended to toss his suitcase in the room, then head out. It seemed so simple. It wasn't. Right across the street was a block-long brick building with a large sign. ***Gibson***. Not merely a business sign. He couldn't pass this up like he'd done in Nashville. This was a sure signal from the Creator. No sooner had he installed himself in the room than he was across the street and inside, touring the hollow- and semi-hollow body guitar factory.

Amazed by the craftsmanship involved, and the customer-focused caring, he ordered a cherry red ES-335. To be shipped to his Big Bear home. His wife would approve, he felt certain. Especially when he showed her the name he'd specified to be custom inserted into the head stock. Hers.

A short walk to the river, and he was steaming down the Mississippi. He imagined standing on the deck, his arm around her, and the world would be in perfect order.

His phone rang.

"Hello, Jack. I'm in Memphis. But I'm sure you know that."

"I have you up on satellite visual right now. Wave."

Micmac waved, but with just one finger. "I'm having a good time, Jack. When do I get Phoebe back?"

"That's one of the two reasons I'm calling. I talked to the Bureau, and they're saying it's going to be a couple more days. Or so."

"What *or so*, Jack? I'm missing her, and we've got a baby to get back to."

"Roger that. Can't be helped. Oh, and the second reason I called. Since you've got a couple of extra days, I need you to get out to the northwest and lend your weapons expertise to Mag. It's all arranged."

"What *arranged*?" He gave it a second. "I'll do it, of course. Can you let Phoebe know?"

"No can do. Still blacked out in Louisville. I'll let you know as soon as the darkness lifts. Okay?"

"Ack. I still had a couple things on my list, but this'll work out. I'll be able to get back here with Phoebe. Keep in touch, Jack. She's important to me."

"Wilco, my man. Will comply. Jack out."

Click.

An hour later Micmac was checked out and on his way to the Memphis airport. Next stop, a place called Yakima. In the state of Washington.

The former SEAL's mind was a mess. He didn't have any manner of a *read in* on Crayle's op and had no idea how he could help. Perhaps that was a characteristic he'd not observed in himself. The ability to enter something blind, and make the best of it.

On the flight west, he thought about his fellow team members.

He thought of Mag, of Hekka, of Lenny, of Alona.

He thought of the little one. How they'd raise her. How quickly she'd be able to unload a Glock .45 caliber semi-automatic pistol into the ten-ring. He smiled.

He thought of Phoebe.

CHAPTER 14

The Crayle team's Falcon 7X jet dropped Lenny and Alona at the Portsmouth, New Hampshire airport. They didn't have to survive the rigors of car rental since a brand new GMC Denali SUV with encrypted comms awaited them at curbside. The driver stowed their bags, handed Lenny the proximity keys, and disappeared into the crowd.

Lenny grinned. "Jack's taking care of us once again."

"Are you kidding? This has Darryl written all over it." She glanced up at the sky. "Thank you, Darryl."

At that moment, a race-clad cyclist blasted by on the Arrivals roadway.

"I wonder . . ." Lenny mused.

Within the hour, they'd checked into the Holiday Inn for a night's stay. A quick refresh and Lenny had them off to Portsmouth's shopping district for some window shopping and a pitcher of beer at one of the local pubs.

• • •

The next day, they repacked and headed north to a place Lenny referred to as Bretton Woods. "It's the location of a famous international money conference."

"You're kidding. You brought me all this way, without our kid, to some beyond boring place?"

"Just wait."

She did. And saw her reward as they approached from the highway. There stood an immense white building with red tile roof. At its highest aspects, it stood seven stories tall.

"Wow. That is gorgeous. Those money types know how to pick their conference venues."

"Yeah. And the money folks get their customers to pay for it all. And look beyond. In the distance you can see Mount Washington. At 6,288.2 feet, it's the tallest peak around. We'll be climbing to the top."

"No, we're not. I like the view from here."

"I didn't mean walk. There's an old cog railway train that takes us up the western slope of the mountain. You'll see. Trust me."

Alona had some doubts until his final two words. Now, she worried.

"We're pre-checked in."

He turned left.

"Wait, Lenny. The resort was dead ahead."

"We're in the Villas." He pulled up to a large, white, two-story house, and they were inside and unpacked in twenty minutes.

Alona stretched out on the bed and immediately fell asleep.

"That's okay," Lenny said. "We'll tour the big resort later. Have some dinner. Agreed?"

Alona said nothing.

"Agreed."

He followed suit and fell asleep next to her.

• • •

When they awoke, it was morning.

"Rise and shine."

They found breakfast in the big building, then hit the road. They drove 3.9 miles, according to Lenny's reading of the car's odometer, to the cog railway station at the base of the mountain. Lenny proceeded to the ticket office. He was sure the young man at the counter would help.

"Tickets for Mr. and Mrs. Lipschitz?"

The young man chuckled. "No. But I have an envelope marked *Shitzlips*." He laughed harder as if it was funny.

As usual, Lenny was armed. His prized straight-from-EBay Walther PPK. He considered whether the seven-shot magazine was sufficient. "I'll take that." He snatched the envelope. "And keep the day job. You'll live longer."

He checked. The name on the envelope was correct. "Some people have warped senses of humor, Alona. Right?"

"I couldn't agree with you more."

Lenny checked the tickets. "There are two. That's a good start. What's this? NO REFUND. NO EXCHANGES. TREAT TICKET AS CASH. Good thing I married an attorney."

"Good thing you married *this* attorney."

"We've got fifty minutes before the train up. Let's buy souvenirs for the team. In the gift shop."

"After. You'll have me packing them around."

"*Moi?*"

"*Vous.*"

They purchased their items, reminisced away the rest of the time over some beer, then ambled out to the loading platform. Just as well. Alona had been 86'd when she'd ordered her third bottle.

Strangely, when they walked to their loading site, there were no other people. Nor any conductors to tell them where to sit. They just boarded, entered the empty car, and found a seat.

"This is an old cog train like they have in Switzerland. A giant gear works a strip of steel teeth that runs between the tracks. The incline up the mountain, according to my brochure, is 37 degrees. That's steep."

"And, as old trains have it, the bench seats are hard wood and the train pulls itself up the mountain at only five miles per hour."

"Hey. I'm a spy now. I'm the intel man here."

She closed the gap to him and whispered, "I'm a spy, too."

"Spies know when to be quiet."

"As they silently snuff out the offending party."

"You're channeling Pattie."

"No. You're wrong. She's a psychopath. I'm an attorney."

"You can explain the difference another time. Oh, look alongside the train tracks. Coming up, a flat rock with a bunch of coins on top."

"And you can tell the difference between that and ..."

He opened the window, and pitched a quarter toward the rock. "Bingo! It didn't bounce off. Portends good luck for our trip today."

"Portends?"

"That's a Mag word."

"See that you spend more time with him."

"Whine."

The two were quiet for a bit, then Lenny broke the silence.

"I like you and alcohol. Makes me romantic."

"Now?"

"There's no one around. And it's a long way to the top."

"You want me to lie on this rock hard wood bench seat?"

He grinned. "Works for me."

"It's not your back."

"True. I should be fine."

"I'm glad to see you have a sensitive side."

"Yeah, well—"

"Look over there!"

He did. Another flat rock.

Further up the track, catastrophe struck.

A sharp crack came from nearby as an errant lightning bolt struck.

Alona reacted by squeezing the bottle of water in her hand. The paper-thin plastic ruptured, drenching her.

"Those ... those so-called environmentalists! Use less plastic, huh!" She flipped her unencumbered middle finger at the surrounding environment.

"What if there were other passengers?"

"You'd say, *It's okay. She's an attorney.*" She gave it a second. "The people would nod, and continue on their way."

He turned to her. "You know, my bottle explodes when you squeeze it like that."

He laughed so hard that, this time, he snorted.

Alona stopped brushing the excess water from her clothes. She tilted back her head to stare skyward. "What did I do?"

CHAPTER 15

At the top of the cog railway, Lenny led the way. The Lipschitz duo climbed from the rail car onto a platform.

The wind picked up from the west, causing Alona to look in that direction. "Looks like a storm coming, Lenny. Remember the warm clothing I wanted to bring?"

Lenny studied his weather app. "Look. If you turn around 360 degrees, you can see how many different directions there are. Storms only come from two of them."

"But..."

"It's true they had a record snowfall of around forty-nine inches, but that was way back in 1969."

"But..."

"No problem. My weather app says we're fine. For a while, at least."

They proceeded uphill to the left of a large visitor pavilion.

Alona pointed dead ahead. "Look at that sign!"

"Yeah. My app has that covered, too. They did measure a world record wind speed of 231 miles per hour, but Australia beat that one in 1996, it says here."

In the short time they'd been there, the wind had accelerated to a howl.

"You seem to be freezing. Let's shelter in that cabin up at the top."

As they approached the moderate sized one-room cabin, Alona pointed to the side. "The sign says Summit. We're at the very top."

"Let's get inside."

They entered the cabin to find a couple of round tables and chairs, as well as a long conference table with chairs. They took a seat.

Through the windows, they viewed trees being nearly bent in half by the gale force winds.

Then came the little white flakes. The few at first upgraded into a full strength snowstorm.

"We might be here for a while, a long while. How about checking the kitchen cabinets over there for some grub?"

As she rose to go look for a butcher knife or something even bigger and sharper, the cabin door blew open. Lenny and Alona jumped. They hadn't seen anyone outside the whole time they'd been on Mount Washington.

Along with the tempest, two women barged inside. They pivoted and, with all of their strength, pushed it closed. They brushed off snow and slowly turned.

"It's okay, ladies," Lenny said. "It's nice and—" He stopped.

The two before them were unmistakable with respect to identification.

"Heidi and Astrid!" Lenny gasped. He remembered the two he'd connected with to set up crypto currency access for the team. He also remembered their presence at the Australian Red Centre's underground death trap. In the company of the Australian Illuminé chief and his Feral henchmen. As the six Crayle team members became the epicenter for the evil man's three mini-nuclear bombs.

“Those Swiss names are fake. They told us so. Their true names are French. Crystel and Alice. Lalumière’s daughters.”

The verbal quiescence that followed did nothing to diminish the howl outside.

Lenny broke a long silence. “This can’t be a coincidence.”

The elder sister, Crystel, said, “We escaped the Red Centre of Australia. We regretted what appeared to be your fate. But our father was Illuminé. We were obedient.”

“That’s right,” Alice added. “When we heard that the directional bombs exploded out rather than in, and that all six of you survived, we decided to make things right with you.” She opened her purse and handed Lenny a small envelope. “Here. This contains your crypto code and a Website name. Login with the ID, Water Diamonds, and you will be asked for the code. Enter it. Once verified, you can choose the amount in any currency, and route it anywhere you wish.”

“That sounds a little too good to be true. Look. Somehow you tracked us here. Now you give us this. What is next?”

Before they could answer, a tremendous sound came from outside. They all ran to windows and used swaths of fabric to wipe away some of the frost. There, outside, a huge Tucker Sno-Cat pulled to a stop. Eight armed men clad in mountain tactical gear jumped out into the wind and cold. They began to fire at the cabin.

The denizens inside ducked to the floor. Lenny and Alona pulled their sidearms. Against AK-47 carbines, they were no match.

Lenny turned to Crystel. “I don’t suppose you have a bazooka or something similar in that tight dress.”

“Just pistols like yours.” Crystel whispered something to her sister.

“Swell.” He turned to Alona to say goodbye. She looked past him with an expression of horror. “No! Don’t!”

The two young women dashed out the door.

Severe gunfire laid down by the attackers took them both out in a couple of seconds.

Lenny peeked. “They’re heading our way. If they were after us, they think they got us. With that storm and with the visibility so impaired, there's no way they could ID the two targets they had, let alone the bodies. This storm is getting much worse. It could set a new world record."

"Forget that, Lenny. Get ready with your weapon. I think eight of them with automatic weapons is eight too many. I just wish I could hold our son one more time."

The storm's strength, and its attendant evil screeching and wailing, was interrupted.

"What's that?"

"It sounds like a . . ."

"It sounds just like one of the Falcons we trek around in."

"They wouldn't fly in this weather."

They both peeked some more.

The sound grew even louder.

The killers glanced to the sky, not believing any pilot would fly in such threatening skies, let alone get so low to the mountain. Any downdraft, and it would surely crash.

They started to scatter.

Too late.

The plane above was indeed one of the Dassault Falcons flown remotely with Micmac's new toy controller. It had something else new. Micmac had replaced the radar-baffling chaff with his weaponized snowflakes. Plastic and steel. Honed to a fine edge.

The white flakes poured out of the starboard bin and into the near hurricane force winds.

Spinning and twirling in all possible directions, they struck the assailants and sliced them to ribbons.

Those that struck the cabin just embedded into the log structure. The machinegun-like ra-ta-tat sounds caused Lenny and Alona to jump.

They'd taken refuge flat on the floor next to a wall. Hearing the screams of the assassins being filleted by the new and heretofore untested flakes, they peeked out the window one more time.

What they saw was a gargantuan storm moving on. And what they also saw was a sea of red in the virgin snow.

They could tell. All of the men were dead.

Lenny turned and sat against the wall. His wife followed suit.

"Alona?"

"What?"

"Remember that coin I landed on the flat rock on the way up? That lucky rock?"

Alona checked outside. "We're stuck here, Lenny. There's no activity at the train stop, and there's like two feet of snow out there."

"Not to mention ten dead, perforated, and lacerated bodies."

"Well, we attorneys never give up. There's also a Snow Cat. Can you drive one?"

"Oh, yeah. It was part of my driving test at the DMV."

She tugged on his arm. "C'mon. We can take warm jackets and stuff off any of the deceased that approximate our sizes."

"Good idea. And, working together, we can get the Cat down that snow-covered road."

"We'll manage. We always do."

"Alona? The bodies?"

"Call in one of those cleanup crews the CIA has."

"Let me check my phone directory."

He noticed a change come over his wife. Excited. As in having scored an epiphany.

"No, Lenny. Call the president."

CHAPTER 16

Crayle hoped their off-the-books travel arranger, Darryl, had been well compensated. He had apparently been instructed to take a circuitous route by a GPS system utilizing artificial intelligence. Designed specifically to expose a single or multiple tails. Crayle recalled their man in Nova Scotia informing him that the system was just at the alpha test stage. He was the guinea pig. And feedback would be appreciated if, indeed, the spy survived. "Swell," Crayle thought out loud. "Anything for the team."

The episode began when Marli set down ex-husband Jack Sommer's Falcon 8X at Portland International Airport in Oregon. With a very special backpack tossed over his shoulder, Crayle deplaned into a chilly, but otherwise fine Fall day. Good visibility in all directions. He was amazed at the fuss the president was making for this informative meet at Hanford. He concluded that the man he would meet there was someone quite special.

His transportation Towne Car's video capability provided a panorama of visuals to spot tails or unusual interest. They arrived at the Hotel Eastlund, and he checked into a fine two bedroom suite.

He'd already showered and changed attire on the plane so he followed the GPS dictation in his ear. It was a short two block walk to a street called Holladay and the tram, which carted him across Portland to the famous Japanese Gardens.

A beautiful place. His Japanese experience was limited to a short stay on the island of Hokkaido—part of an exfil route—so the variety of flora and the ponds were new. And restful. He made a mental note to someday check out the rest of that far eastern country, but with Hekka. And their child. And with no mission to accomplish.

So far, no sign of a tail.

After a quick cup at the Tea House, he threaded his way through the voluminous Powell's City of Books, searching for his own novel, The Water Diamonds. No luck. Disappointment took him to the Rock Bottom Brewery.

In short order, he returned on the rail loop. He didn't stop at the hotel. All along he glanced into windows, checking for followers. None. So far.

A street later he was directed to the right onto the indigenous-sounding Multnomah Street. Down a couple of blocks he arrived at Lloyd Center, entered the Stanford's Restaurant and Bar, and ordered the AI-specified lunch.

The computer must have worked up quite an appetite. Or thought Crayle was a party of four. The Kruse Burger stood a healthy four inches high. The stack of beer-battered onion rings stood elbow to fingertip high. He washed down the Creole Crab Cakes with a Deschutes Black Butte Porter to finish it all off. He considered it a good thing he had about a four block return walk to the hotel. Crayle paid the bill, tipped well, and trekked back, carefully considering the benefits of a two or three hour nap.

The food at Stanford's was excellent. He made a note. "Excellent food and nice ambience. Come back here."

Even though he'd been in the open most of the day, the GPS instructions started to feel confining. They should just get a robot, he thought.

Back at the Hotel Eastlund, he queried his Darryl device. Up to the outdoor bistro called Altabira for a dry vodka martini with a twist. Shaken. Not stirred. Perfect. He felt like a spy again.

• • •

The next morning, as he checked out of the hotel, he accepted a small box the clerk handed to him. The GPS, seemingly in control of his life, directed him to his car in the garage, where he utilized the keys from the box. This was getting tiresome except he remembered what not tiresome meant in his profession and accepted the reprieve, no matter how brief.

"Head east on 84 along the south side of the Columbia River." The GPS thought for a second. "Oh, here. I'll drive."

Crayle pulled his hands off the wheel. That he had much more time to surveille for followers was of little consolation.

He wanted badly to talk to Hekka, but the president had expressly ordered a communication blackout. For the duration of the op.

As if reading his mind, the GPS introduced itself. "Hello, I'm Hekka Crayle." What he heard caused him to grab the wheel only to receive a shock. He pulled back.

"Just thought you'd like a friendly voice, so I'm it. An exact match, synthesized voice replica derived from the voice recognition analysis team at Science and Technology."

"What if I'm not Magus Crayle?"

"Oh, he wants to play. Okay. Then, I'm to assume you are Mr. Phelps. And inform you that your car will destroy itself in five seconds. Hmmm?"

"Some sense of humor."

"Who's joking?"

"Where to?"

"Just to the north, we have Mount Saint Helens."

He observed what was left of the mountain. "Another day."

The voice provided tourist-like dialog while making surveillance stops at the Vista House lookout point, then Bonneville Dam and Cascade Locks. Finally, near a place called The Dalles, they crossed the Columbia River into Washington state.

"Finally."

"Patience, Mr. Crayle. I am now proceeding onto Highway 97, across the mid-Washington desert, to the beautiful town, Toppenish. As you will have noticed by now from the signage, we've entered the Yakama Indian Reservation."

"Now there's a real live connection to Hekka. You probably know she's Serrano."

"Yes. I have an entire data base on the both of you."

"Will you look at that?" Crayle said in awe.

"You must be viewing the extensive wall murals depicting the history. People come from around the world to see them. They're all over the town."

"You're becoming like an old friend. I know you're not Hekka. So, what's your name?"

"Pattie."

"Not funny."

"Ah, we're here. This is the Legends Casino. Go inside. Play the poker slot machine. Ten hands at a time. Maximum bet. I'll pick you up when you're done."

With no choice, he did as instructed. He found the Ten Play machine and sat down. Shortly, an older woman took the seat beside him. Her features indicated an indigenous parentage.

"Hi. Having any luck?"

"Just started."

She made the same all in bet as he did, drew the five cards, and hit pay dirt. A Royal Flush. On the draw. A button press later, and the ten hands each paid the highest possible return. She cashed out.

"You could make even more by selling some of that luck to the rest of us."

She smiled. "Your luck is about to change."

He looked back at the machine, and then at her. She was gone.

Crayle played again. Royal Flush. All ten hands. He followed her lead and printed out his winnings. There, on the ticket, were instructions. For tomorrow.

Outside, the driverless car awaited. It proceeded north to the town of Yakima and its Best Western Plus accommodations. Crayle was very tired. After he checked into his room, he didn't even change for bed. The Yakima Herald-Republic newspaper on the coffee table would be good for some local flavor. In the morning. Sleep came quickly.

CHAPTER 17

The next morning began with a bang. In the living room. Crayle jumped from the bed, SIG-Sauer .40 in hand. Not wanting to backlight himself, he left the lights off. He carried a Mag light in his free hand, at arms length to the side, ready to flip on and blind an opponent.

From beside the door frame, he pushed open the bedroom door. Then spun as he lit off the flashlight. Modern LED bulbs where uber bright. They could disorient someone not prepared.

Not seeing anyone at first, he stepped forward. And tripped.

An end table lamp flashed on.

Crayle pushed his light and weapon in that direction.

"Hi, Mag. It's me. Micmac. Uh, don't shoot."

There, having defeated the door lock, he'd snuck in and slept on the couch, and then fallen off. There lay the former SEAL.

"I could have taken you out. Are you crazy?"

"Just a little. The president decided I had some free time while Phoebe finishes out her extended stay in Louisville. You know, two minds listening to the same intel, then comparing notes. Good idea."

"As long as you stay alive. Please, don't do that again."

"Roger that. And Wilco. I will comply."

"I received instructions at a nearby casino. Let's get ready and head out. First a town southeast called Richland. Then Hanford. And the B Reactor."

He made sure to have the backpack when they departed.

• • •

The two men checked into the Richland, Washington office for the Manhattan Project National Historical Park, and were shown to an extended GMC SUV. Crayle recognized the driver right away. From the casino.

"Good morning, messieurs Crayle and MacKay. I'm Mrs. X."

The woman of few words drove them alongside the western boundary of the Hanford area, then east, turning right at a guard shack. Papers in order, they proceeded to the decommissioned B Reactor complex. The trio exited the parked SUV, with the two men following Mrs. X into the main building.

It looked the part, as far as they knew, of a reactor facility. At least, there were no windows on any of the gray cement sides.

She led them past an array of fans, valves, and pumps and into a squared-off room. A number of rows of inexpensive chairs faced a large cube before them.

They turned to face an stumpy old man with white frizzy hair. While not quite passing for Albert Einstein, he did look the aged scientist part. He also matched the description of the nuclear physicist Crayle had received from President Stones.

"That, gentlemen, is the reactor core. The pile, or collection of tubes, graphite blocks, radioactive materials, water cooling, et cetera, is right there. Or was. It's no longer active. Taken down in February of 1968. You are quite safe."

"I'd feel safe about three hundred miles from here," Micmac noted.

"You see this backpack, Doctor?" Crayle extracted Lenny's bomb. From New Zealand.

The sight of it struck the doctor hard. "That is the mini-nuke device." He rubbed his hand over the textured surface. "It truly emits no radiation?"

"And absorbs it when the bomb explodes. Do you have anything to tell us about this?"

There was a protracted moment of silence as the old scientist looked from man to man and then back at the bomb.

"It's time I spoke." He glanced over at his wife, who just shook her head. "It turns out that the radiation sponge was invented right here."

"At Hanford?"

"Ah," he sighed. "Right here."

Crayle's mind shifted to high gear. He was sure where the conversation was likely to lead, but needed the man to supply the details freely. "We are cleared by the president. And I believe you've held onto this for quite a while. It's time for you to unload."

X had indeed. "While we developed the weapons-grade plutonium, we would discuss not only the devastation of the atomic weapons created in Los Alamos, but the radioactive contamination making the surrounding area a dead zone for many, many years."

"And that led you to an antidote?"

"The radiation sponge was developed toward that end. But there was a major hurdle. We put the idea on the shelf. For several years."

"And then, a breakthrough?"

"Yes, Mr. Crayle. You are quite insightful."

Crayle observed as the man peered down at his fingers, interlaced on the table edge. "It was you?"

A sigh. Then, "You are correct again. We, of high intellect and knowledge, had over thought the problem, impeding progress on the last impediment."

"A common failing of collections of geniuses."

"My solution was elegant ... and perfect."

"The paisley-like construction of the sponge? Was that the secret?"

"It held the secret. The variable-width air gaps in a manner embodying the Yin and Yang."

"That your bombs would kill tens or hundreds of thousands at a shot, but leave the target area inhabitable for a massive cleanup and reoccupation made it okay?"

"Washington, D.C. would decide the where and the when. And the morality."

Crayle fully understood the transference of guilt ploy. He'd done it himself. As Crayle Two. After creating a master geopolitical strategy that employed nuclear devices. "It was never deployed by the US, was it? Why?"

"I'd scribbled the science on a blackboard. We did that whenever we created a new idea. That way, the rest could see our logic, and produce questions or propose improvements. The high five hadn't been invented, so we shook hands at the wondrous achievement. We left for the lunch room to take a break. On the way back, we passed one of the janitors. I noted that he was in a place outside of his normal routine."

"Did you track him down or report your observation to security?"

"One of us remembered that an 'impromptu' inspection was but an hour away."

"Impromptu? As in surprise?"

"Government, Mr. Crayle. Government."

"Can we get you some water, Dr. X?"

"I continue."

"Let me know if you need a break. This is some heady intel."

"Thank you. The next day, I checked on him."

"The janitor."

"Yes. He … no. His landlord had called in sick for him. At this point, you could say I panicked. I asked security to check on him. Short version, he was gone. No trace at hospitals, bus stations, or airports. Nothing on taxi logs. Car still on street in front of his apartment complex."

"Excluding that he somehow escaped by boat or alien abduction … "

"Security found film negatives at his residence. We examined them and all jaws dropped. There were pictures of formulae we'd scribbled on the black board, but had erased before we'd left the room."

"I'm guessing here. He had a special camera, then. It could pick up the artifacts of the erasures. Before he used his military-specification cleaning liquid to fully erase the marks."

"Yes, Mr. Crayle. Correct. We had a very good mathematician on our team, but we could have used your powers of perception."

"What did you do?"

"We destroyed the board."

An epiphany struck. He couldn't let Dr. X know what he knew about the mini-nukes. "What was this janitor's ethnicity?"

"White as the mid-Winter snow."

Crayle scowled. "There goes that idea."

"The adopted son of Chinese immigrants."

Crayle's head snapped around. "Chinese? You're certain?"

"Absolutely. They'd escaped the communist repression in China. Thoroughly vetted."

"By the same government which schedules 'surprise' inspections that everyone knows about in advance?"

"The prospective parents were examined very carefully prior to the adoption. Model citizens."

"Where from in China?"

"Some place near Shanghai. That's all I know."

Yes, Crayle thought to himself. Some place near Shanghai. Where they made the radiation-suppressed mini-nukes.

CHAPTER 18

Phoebe remained in Louisville, impatiently waiting for her 'minor' FBI op to commence. For something requiring her skill set right away, she noted a definite hurry up and wait government smell associated with it. She wanted her Smartphone to ring and her husband to be on the other end. That would be normal. As it stood, she didn't know if he was in Nashville or Memphis, or stuck somewhere in between.

Comms blackouts were the pits. Phoebe realized the rationale for them, but wanted more than anything to hook up with her husband, in an all senses of the word hookup. The silence from her Smartphone deafened. She waited and waited and waited, with only a few Kentucky Bourbon interludes.

She wondered. Had Micmac gotten to sit in with a band in Nashville? Or Memphis? Those would have been keepsake memories for a musician like himself. And what about Magus and Hekka? And Lenny and Alona? She felt she could scream. Or go crazy. Or both.

At long last, Phoebe received the call from her boss's boss. The lead on the minor 'piece of cake' operation in Louisville, Kentucky.

“It’s a go,” he said. “Green light.” He provided the surveillance target’s name, and went farther. “He’s on the sixth floor.” He provided the room number. Then, “Wait! I’ve got hotel surveillance up . . . someone’s breaking into his room! MacKay! Get up there now!”

Phoebe picked up the just cleaned Glock 30, racked the slide. She pushed it into an inside-the-waistband holster, and shoved that under the back of her blouse to its place at the small of her back. A quick draw from concealment would have her left hand pull the blouse hem up, and the right withdraw the weapon. For draw, aim, and fire, she’d been clocked at six tenths of a second. In a tie for the world record.

Phoebe wanted badly to call Micmac and tell him that the ‘soft’ op had gone the other way. She was dark, under orders, and that was not an option.

The elevator seemed to take forever as it ignored her. “C’mon. C’mon. C’mon!”

Sixth floor. She peeked out. No one in sight. Numbers on the wall indicated which direction.

She moved slowly with her hands at her back, but not drawing the Glock. In case an innocent bystander stepped out of their room. Panicky collaterals never helped.

There it was. Sixth floor. Room 66. Her mind put it together. 666.

It was good not to have been raised in a superstitious family.

A metal toggle safety device installed to limit door openings to a few inches, so the occupant could see who was knocking outside, propped the door open so the built-in spring couldn’t shut the door. One safety feature defeating the other. Odd. A clear security violation for the party or parties inside.

For a brief second, Phoebe thought of her baby. She’d never been a mother in a lock and load situation.

Then, the sound of an excruciating gasp through the door gap.

Phoebe drew her .45 caliber Glock 30, checked the chamber, and pushed through the door.

She'd had a few jaw dropping experiences since she'd joined the Crayle team. None like this one.

There, facing the end of a bed, stood a lanky muscular man. Naked. Just in front of him, a half-dressed form on the bed. On hands and knees. It was sex. That kind of sex.

He glanced at the intruder, and spoke. "Wrong room?"

"No! Drop your weapon!"

The black and white clad diminutive woman receiving the man's efforts turned her head toward the FBI Agent.

Phoebe gasped.

"*Pattie!*"

Before Phoebe could zero in with her signature between-the-eyes shot, Pattie swung her French Manurhin pistol from beneath the pillow.

That a silencer was already attached was all Phoebe needed to know. A setup.

Pattie fired.

Pffft. Pffft.

The high-velocity Plus-P rounds slammed Phoebe against the door frame.

Once again, images flashed in her mind. Micmac. Her new baby.

Then, nothing.

She fell forward, hitting the floor hard.

Patti Norbrunn, the CIA's most rogue agent ever, returned the weapon under the pillow.

She turned, looking over her shoulder at the astonished male prostitute. Some aspiring singer-songwriter trying to earn enough to seek fame and fortune a few hours south in Nashville.

"Finish me!" she commanded.

Instead of doing as ordered, he grabbed his clothes. Then, he stopped.

He peered back at his employer. She had the gun back in her hand. Pointed at him.

There would be no Nashville.

He didn't hear the shot.

Slowly, softly, Pattie stepped off the bed and shook the nun's habit down over her legs.

She moved to Phoebe's body.

• • •

Pattie had taken down Phoebe with a 7.65 millimeter pistol. "Don't need a .45 cannon."

She knelt next to the body for a moment before stroking Phoebe's blonde hair. Then, she lifted the braid Phoebe wore next to her left temple. In her father's memory. She massaged it between her thumb and forefinger.

"Why couldn't I have had *your* father? Why couldn't I have had normal honor? Integrity? Why couldn't I have been your sister?" She stopped for a moment. "Sleep well."

She clutched her rosary beads in one hand, her gold cross in the other. And closed her eyes. "Forgive me, Father, for I have sinned… again."

• • •

It was later. Pattie had just finished throwing up in the bathroom. She rinsed her mouth and brushed her teeth. Back in the bedroom, she once again knelt beside the body.

Her hand reached for the braid now dangling toward the floor. Almost with respect, she bent and kissed the flesh next to where it began. "I could have loved you, darling. And Hekka, too. Here." She pulled the long leg sheath from her cross to reveal the razor-sharp, four-inch blade, and cut the braid free. "I'll keep this for a while. To remember you by."

She replaced the sheath and made the sign of the cross. "Forgive me, Father." She stood. "Oh, hell." She glanced upward, waving her hand at the ceiling. "You know the routine by now."

Pattie stood and engaged her Smartphone. She instructed that a cleanup team be dispatched. Her directions were for them to transfer the bodies onto the bed. She mentioned that she'd noticed some fluids near the man's private parts, and that the cleaners needed to transfer a small amount to the Agent. She clicked off.

"There. Rough sex gone bad."

She brushed off her hand prints and placed the pistol in his, assuring finger print evidence other than her own. A quick rub of the back of her gun hand on his provided gunshot residue to back up the fake murder-suicide scene.

Pattie bent close to Phoebe. "It's all right, sweetheart. Micmac is very smart. He'll know you weren't with another man. He'll come after me. Maybe I'll show him some love before I do him. And the others. You'll all meet up in that Heaven place. I won't be there. You'll miss me."

She made the sign of the cross. "Sleep well, pretty Phoebe."

Clearly, Pattie had crossed the boundary into psychosis some time ago. She'd killed too many to list. They'd just become *et cetera* when the subject came up with her husband.

And she wasn't finished.

CHAPTER 19

One short hop from Richland, Washington, to Seattle and a refuel later, Crayle and side-kick Micmac flew west over the Pacific Ocean. With hours to kill, small talk seemed the best escape from the gravity of what they'd learned in Hanford. It boiled down to the thousands who'd already perished from the miniature nuclear devices, which could turn out to be a small down payment for the mayhem ahead. With Flori Sommers up front in the pilot's seat of the Dassault Falcon 7X, they lounged in the sumptuous white leather chairs in the cabin, facing each other. Crayle initiated the conversation.

"Small talk?"

"Yeah," Micmac responded. "I should've known I'd miss Phoebe as much as I do. The blacked out comms, due to her mission and our mission, are driving me crazy. I just know I should've stayed with her in Louisville."

"Trust me, she's fine. All those years she spent protecting key witnesses in cases against very dangerous criminals. No one can survive like Phoebe Bransfield MacKay. Anyway, her FBI boss told her it was a piece-of-cake op and not to worry."

"I met the guy once. Wasn't too sure about him, but I've been wrong in first impressions more than a few times."

Crayle smiled. "How 'bout them Indians?"

"You mean Hekka? And the Serrano?"

"No, Micmac. Small talk. The Cleveland Indians."

The former SEAL scrunched his face. "They have Indians way up there?"

They both allowed a smile. Then, a chuckle. Then, a laugh.

Crayle pressed a button on the CIA Universal Remote next to his sumptuous leather seat. It reclined flat. "Let's rest up. Hong Kong's going to be busy."

• • •

Pilot Flori landed the 7X as softly as she spoke. She provided the men suitable passports, but stepped back when Crayle invited her along. "Might be here a few days," he advised her. "I'll fill you in on the imperial protocols on the way to the palace. Empress Ling will be providing transport, so anything we say should be guarded. The Imperial Palace is fully bugged, as well."

"You already know I'm a trained and experienced international operative. Jack and I have history to that end. In Brazil."

"And you married him, anyway. I'll have a chat with the man."

"He'll just want to talk about the sex. You know, brag."

Crayle knew that, given the opportunity, the Brazil sexual Flori would go into detail next. "Oh, look outside. Our ride's here."

• • •

Inside the Imperial Palace perched above Hong Kong city, Ling received the call she expected. Crayle and MacKay had arrived at the Lantau airport on the eponymous island just west, and their passports were in order. Closer inspection, per orders, was not necessary. She knew they'd be armed. But, would that be sufficient to protect her from Yellow? And all of her other adversaries.

Forty minutes later, they all sat in the palace welcoming chamber. Ling quickly took a liking to Flori, introduced as their pilot, happy she didn't need to compete with the cleavage or the warm sexiness innate to the Brazilian woman.

"By the way, it's okay to say anything in front of her. She's sworn to silence." Crayle indicated Flori.

"Things are serious here. My agents provided the following intel. The old communist party's Standing Committee, the remnants of which I have running the country, seeks the means to a coup. The mini-nukes, as you refer to them, fit that need."

"If I follow, they just need one to take out this palace."

"And every one inside."

"And, I'm afraid, the rest of Hong Kong."

Ling nodded at the seriousness of that potential. "Although I didn't have them imprisoned or executed, they're still communists at heart. Compelled by an ideology."

Micmac and Flori schooled up on the young empress and her situation. They both noted the confluence of poise and youth. They were impressed. They remained silent, per Crayle's instructions.

"With the new directional weapons, they might be able to remove this palace with little or no impact on Hong Kong city. And all the wealth they'd need to preserve."

Ling reached for a dangling, thick ribbon, and pulled. White daughter walked in through hanging drapes. "Yes?"

"Please prepare refreshments for our guests, White." She turned to Micmac and Flori and, with a sweeping gesture, said, "Please."

The two rose and followed White from the room.

Ling turned to Crayle. "I've something to show you, Magus."

She pressed a remote control button and an ancient wall painting turned into a video screen.

"Are you familiar with the wine auctions, Magus?"

"Of course. Fine wines are auctioned off to rich folks. They are then challenged to either drink the wines, as an ego salve, or the keep them and watch them increase in value. The problem is so severe, many are driven to suicide."

"I forgot your sense of humor. Any way, Hong Kong has now surpassed New York for the number one spot in these auctions."

"That, my dear Ling, is a surprise. So what do you have there on your computer screen?"

"This is Chinese wine country."

"Chinese what?"

The young empress frowned an admonishment.

"This one sits away from the seven regions known to outsiders for their viticulture. Those include Ninxia whose wines have bested Bordeaux in blind tests."

"I'm impressed. Developing vineyards takes a long time."

"Wine was transported here long ago from territories far to the west. Central Asia. Modern Uzbekistan. Marco Polo even mentioned a wine-growing area in Xinjiang."

"Yes. Chin had Li transport a mini-nuke out there as part of my Blackstone Strategy. I doubt the people in the Ürümqi capitol were concerned about the wine growing when their primary city turned into a mushroom cloud."

"Point taken."

"Nowadays, wine growing and production requires modern techniques. We've perfected them."

"My predecessors acquired the technology for successful growth from your Napa Valley region of California."

"I'm impressed with the quality of your satellites, Ling."

"Actually, they're yours."

"We would call that theft, but continue."

"The communists decried all that was capitalism, but knew for certain that the latter ideology was a necessary money pump. They couldn't afford to develop technologies. Only steal them."

"I'm familiar with the showstopper shortcomings of the radical and extreme left."

"Look closer. Notice anything odd?"

"The workers harvesting the grapes look a bit artificial." He stopped. "Robots?"

"Very good. China whined and whined about not having natural resources. We created numerous mines. We knew there was nothing to be found. We developed highly sophisticated robotics in underground factories."

"Let me guess. With the aid of stolen Japanese technology."

"Stolen is a harsh word."

"Pejorative, too."

"*Touché*."

"There's more?"

"It's what's beneath the small plateau of the vineyards."

"Of course! You're bringing in uranium via the mine network. Enriching. And building the mini-nukes. The river water that appears as mere irrigation for the crops actually cools the enriched isotopes. But our surveillance satellites just see vineyards."

"Our wines were engineered not to compete with yours. Not an economic threat."

"You don't miss much, do you?"

"We can't afford to." She stood, and offered her hand. "Come. We join your friends."

"Wait! What's that?"

She turned to the screen.

A caravan of four black SUVs drove up the unpaved road to the vineyards.

Ling grabbed the remote. She pressed ZOOM. "It's them!"

"They're after a bomb!"

Her previous calm demeanor transformed to terrified. "What do I do?"

"When it's my turn, I've got something to show *you*. Let's keep an eye on this scene."

Micmac walked back into the room. The large, wall-sized video caught his eye. "So, what's up?"

CHAPTER 20

Several hundred miles west of Hong Kong, fifteen men alighted from the SUV caravan.

The grape harvesting robots paid no attention. Except one. It stood, tipped its hat, then returned to its labor.

The leader of the incursion opened a storage barn door to admit his cohorts. Three sported backpacks.

Back in Hong Kong, the sub-team of three stood in the receiving room with Ling. Crayle fetched his personalized remote control from a hollowed out Holy Bible. It seemed appropriate. In its current state, it contained no religious material. Fitting for those in the video. Perhaps he'd quit his CIA job, hollow out *good books*, and sell them to Illuminé. And other atheists.

He realized his attempt at humor, though not spoken, surpassed that of Lenny, but in the wrong direction. Perhaps he needed some serious therapy. In a spare moment, he'd ask Ling for a reference.

"I need excellent satellite reception. Let's go topside where we have a clear shot up. Here on top of Mount Victoria, there shouldn't be any interference."

He pulled off a HDMI cable from a flat-panel television and attached to it the thumb drive transmitter Micmac had just handed him. Then, he plugged another thumb drive into the TV monitor. The two carted the display unit upstairs. And returned to the video they'd seen downstairs. Micmac initiated his tablet computer, and Crayle provided his observations.

"They went inside, then someone turned out the lights. That implies that they took an elevator down to the nuke factory. Someone saving electricity topside gave that away."

Micmac worked on a tablet computer with his usual intensity. "I'm having a bit of trouble here."

Crayle took a look. "Ling? A little help, please?"

She stepped close to the SEAL. The empress was of moderate height, and kept a figure perfect for the Chinese cheongsam dress she wore on this occasion. Utilizing her beguiling, rounded lips, she said, "We do not have time for you to learn the thousands of Chinese characters. I will assist."

She pressed against his side in order to access the computer screen.

He felt her warmth. And her attraction. "I'm married, you know."

"And I am leader of a country of 1.5 billion people. We both have serious commitments. And keep them at the forefront."

Over the next ten minutes, they went back and forth. He provided the technology decisions, and she the inputs using the Mandarin character set.

"There! I've hacked into their system." He glanced sideways. "Say again, *we've* hacked into their system." He pointed at the application they'd inserted. "Stuxnet II." He referenced a years-ago Israeli hack into Iran's nuclear program.

"When I took power," Ling said. "I threatened to shut down the whole nuclear weapons program. They ..." She pointed toward the screen. "... threatened to blow me up. In no uncertain terms. I left the program alone."

"We can't leave it alone. Micmac, what's the reading on the current batch of their fissile materials?"

"They've got most of it up to atomic number 239. Plutonium. It reads that it's cleaned up. So, weapons grade."

"As we learned at the Hanford site."

Crayle took the tablet computer as Micmac offered it. He pressed a plus sign.

All pairs of eyes bore into the display.

"Heat it up."

"240."

"Getting hot."

They watched.

"Hotter."

"241."

"The cauldron's starting to boil."

"242!"

"We're there!"

"New book idea," Crayle said. "*The Wrath of Grapes*."

He pressed ***PLAY***.

• • •

The destruction of the vineyards played on the state-owned television network. There was nothing left, and explanations from the government were nonexistent. As was the revolutionary element of its leadership. All those at the wine country underground site turned to paste.

The routinely rogue Hong Kong cable station mused how the thousands of grapes had been turned into one mushroom, referring to the nuclear cloud hanging over the epicenter.

Teams were mustered and sent to the region. Those left in charge by the former Standing Committee members looked at the videos and saw Chernobyl. Radiation containment teams were dispatched post haste.

CHAPTER 21

Landing at Dulles International Airport west of America's capitol was normal for Flori Sommers. No one in the American spy service cared that Dulles was named after the long ago Secretary of State, John Foster Dulles. But they did smile when they thought of his brother. Allen Dulles served as Director of Central Intelligence from 1953 to 1961. For them, Reagan National, closer to DC, didn't have that kind of cachet.

Flori taxied to the appropriate Top Secret hangar. Parked, she fetched and disbursed two sweaters and quilted jackets to her passengers. Crayle and Micmac had acclimated to Hong Kong weather. Virginia experienced a cold spell.

Transport and ingress to the Manassas underground lair of the off-the-books Strategic Solutions Office occurred without incident. Or notice. The two men knew their way through the chartreuse passageways.

Crayle punched in the door code for Jack Sommers office. They seated themselves. Sommers strolled in two minutes later.

"Welcome back. That was quite an op in China. I saw the fallout, pun intended, on my video feed. Nice job."

"Unless someone elsewhere has reverse-engineered the mini-nukes, we're done with the supply side of the equation. We're down to those they've sold and distributed."

"They went for many millions apiece. What's Ling and her country going to do to replace the revenue?"

"I foresaw that problem. I gave her some ideas for going forward. Her eyes got real big on the prospects. I'll have to travel back if she wants to move on my suggestions."

"Another topic, then. It seems we've got a coronation scheduled in Paris not far from now. I want the team there. Just in case."

"Just in case? Not likely that Pattie and Lalumière will blow the place up. Not with them in it."

Flori broke the ensuing silence. "How about I go freshen up while you guys talk shop? You know." She turned to her husband. "In the bedroom."

She left via a back door.

"She's good," Micmac observed. "Great pilot."

"She takes Jack where he wants to go," Crayle quipped.

"Having fun at my expense is prohibited under CIA Code 7654321. Okay? Okay. Now, Magus, you'll find Hekka and child out the door and to the left. Three doors down. The access code is the middle three digits of your Social Security number. Backwards."

Crayle departed. He missed them dearly. Now that he'd returned in one piece from Hanford and Hong Kong, he needed to be with them. And perhaps her room led to a bedroom as did Jack's. Little Kianna was going to need a sibling.

Micmac and Jack were the only ones in the room.

"So, where's Phoebe? And our daughter?"

Jack took a moment. Then, a long breath. "She's not here, Micmac."

"She can't still be in Louisville. That's got to be finished by now."

"It is finished."

"I don't like the sound of that."

"I'm sorry."

"Oh, no! No! No! No!" The former SEAL shook his head vigorously. "Don't... don't..." The intensity of the moment was too much. Tears flowed from eyes that had seen the horrors of combat. And had toughed it out.

He jumped up and hefted the chair over his head. He looked for someplace to throw it.

There was Jack. Sitting just feet away.

The former SEAL started toward him.

Jack's eyes got big. He knew he'd just delivered the worst news possible. Was this the end?

Micmac stopped. He set the chair back down, slowly. And lowered himself into it.

Minutes passed before he regained a semblance of control. His world, he felt in his heart, had ended. He hadn't been there at that crucial moment. To protect. To save.

Having finally caught his breath, Jack continued in a soft voice. "I'm hating this part. We received a video." He clicked a remote control.

Micmac witnessed in full color and high-definition what had happened in the Louisville hotel room. Not the doer, just the done.

He was stunned. Devastated. The video left no doubt he'd not see Phoebe alive ever again. He clapped his palms against his eyes. "*No!*"

"As I said, I'm sorry. And I don't have a speech or some platitude for a situation like this one." Jack took a deep breath. Exhaled. "She was the best. The best of the best at the FBI. When I informed President Stones, he only said one word. Arlington."

Micmac recovered a bit. "And I'm away somewhere. Not there to help. With comms blacked out."

"You couldn't know. Your baby's with Hekka. She's filled in Magus by now."

"And her body?"

"Don't have it yet. Her boss is working it."

"He's the one who sent her there!" Micmac pounded the desk. He looked at Jack. "What if he set her up?" He paused as he mulled the possibilities. "What if he's ... Illuminé?"

The former SEAL jumped to his feet and turned. He grabbed the relic Louis XIV chair, spun, and heaved it right at Jack Sommers' head.

It barely missed.

Not a moment too soon, his target launched himself under his desk, spun onto his back, and scrambled for the French Manurhin 9mm Neil Wohlford had kept clipped under the main drawer. Just in case.

Jack fumbled. The adrenaline rush and the knowledge that Neil maintained the weapon loaded and cocked at all times didn't help matters.

He heard a loud crash from behind. Peering out, he observed the damage done.

Loosing very little velocity in transit, the chair had hit Neil's French display cabinet full force. Fine crystal, Baccarat and Lalique, were everywhere. Limoges china had not been spared. In fact, everything Illuminé mole Wohlford once considered dear had been destroyed in a single act.

Slowly, Jack emerged.

He saw no-one at first, and rose.

Micmac stood with his back against the far wall, then slid to a seated position on the floor.

Jack recognized the thousand-yard stare.

"I take it the chair wasn't meant for me. Without my previous boss having been here, and all that meant, Phoebe would still be with us. Is that it?"

Mick MacKay's voice, typically strong, was a mere whisper. "Yeah. That's it."

"And ..."

"Sorry, Jack."

"Sorry you missed?"

"That, too."

"Let's have a drink."

Micmac waved at the destruction at the far end of the room. "Looks like I took down all of Monsieur Wohlford's fine brandy and cognac, too."

Jack opened the bottom right side drawer of the desk. He withdrew a full bottle of Evan Williams Kentucky Straight Bourbon Whiskey, walked over and took a seat next to his bereaved comrade. He held out the bottle. "You got all the glasses. All-in-all, a ten on the Olympic scale for chair heaving."

Micmac unscrewed the top, and took a swig. "It's simple. You drink from the bottle, toss it when you're done. Glasses you have to wash."

The former Navy man had lost a number of military cohorts in combat. But the weight of those losses was no match for this one. He handed over the whiskey.

Jack considered what nearly transpired a few moments before. He took an extra big dose.

CHAPTER 22

As he sat in his underground complex office, SSO head and temporary top dog of the Central Intelligence Agency, Jack Sommers had no more words for his subordinates, Mick MacKay or Magus Crayle, who'd just returned to the office. What happened to Micmac's wife, Phoebe, in Louisville, Kentucky sucked every last bit of oxygen from any further discussion. In brief, their minds had gone blank. And the top player in the espionage sphere required their presence.

"It's time to go, guys. The president wanted a meet. Couldn't say no."

Micmac interrupted his floor stare. "Negats, Jack. Tell him I'm going to spend some time with our kid."

"He's aware of the circumstances. He'll understand. Go."

The former SEAL departed.

Jack pushed up from the floor. "That was the toughest it's ever been."

Crayle inspected the empty whiskey bottle. "I see. I could've used a hit of this, myself."

"C'mon, Mag. Time for us to blast over to Langley in the VacTran. That's our new name for the hyper vacuum tunnel transport system. Three hundred miles per hour, nominal."

"Copping engineering from the Germans. So, the Chinese and the Russians aren't the only ones stealing technology."

"Hey, if you can't beat 'em … "

"Jack, we have to beat them. The game is winner take all. With your skills in the Chinese and Russian languages, or lack thereof, you better fight."

At 300 miles per hour, they arrived at the Langley CIA headquarters in short order. President Stones awaited them in the STIF room.

"Hello, gentlemen." He shook hands. "Have a seat." They did. "I believe you know my personal assistants, Susanna and Luisa." The two women who sat on either side of the president both had history with him. Professional and otherwise. "Susanna, as I believe I've told you before, worked at the San Ernestino newspaper in the marketing department. As you may remember, that's when I was on leave from the NSA. She sees to my public relations now. Luisa was the proofreader. She made my stories, written under the moniker Dexter Freehand, look their best. So be sure to get your grammar and punctuation right. And use strong verbs."

They all nodded and smiled. The president continued.

"Thanks for the job in China, Magus. Nice. No more mini-nukes altering the geopolitical playing field, and the rules."

"Couldn't have done it without Empress Ling."

"I'll have to resume trade negotiations to pay off that debt."

"Don't hurt yourself, Mr. President."

There was a brief smile. "Sorry as hell about Phoebe Bransfield."

"I'll pass it on to Micmac. You know that whole operation had the feel of a set up. Her boss looks good for it."

"You can't go around whacking FBI managers." The president read the look on Crayle's face. "Hey, what are you planning?"

"Can't tell you."

"What? Top Secret? I'm the president, for Chrissakes."

"Plausible deniability. We never discussed it."

"Be careful. Big time. And keep MacKay's feet firmly planted on the ground. We've already lost a good one. We can't afford to lose him."

"As he himself would say, *Ack!*"

"Acknowledged. Great. Uh, look, Magus. I'm giving you and Hekka a full round of absolutely nothing. I know you've wanted to research your father's heritage since the time Doctor Rorschach restored your memories of him. And Hekka. Her Serrano Indian half. She wanted to get out and do some of that indigenous peoples research."

"You've already set things in motion. Who do I contact?"

The president smiled. They both knew the answer.

"Darryl."

CHAPTER 23

Whenever a man of Kimbel Stones' position began with *a president walks into a bar*, one knew the joke was going to be funny. And, later that day, seated before him, Magus and Hekka Crayle were definitely in need of humor.

The president and the Crayles did share a laugh. Then, on to business.

"Like I said, Mag, we need to get you and Hekka out of town for a bit. Ideas?"

"I do. I learned from the latest of Doctor Rorschach's memory restores that my father's Welsh side came to the US, not from Wales, but from a place in Argentina. It's south of Buenos Aires. About halfway down to the tip at Cape Horn."

"Go on."

"A group of Welsh pioneers arrived in 1865 and founded the settlement. My ancestors settled there in 1874."

"I've actually given it some thought, Magus. I know your father was of Welsh heritage. I worked with Jack on this one. I had him dig into the Defense Intelligence Agency archives. They indicated that your dad journeyed to a place in Argentina. Before he went to Asia on his fateful trip, he visited the little Welsh settlement called Gaiman. Near a coastal town, Puerto Madryn."

He stopped to allow questions. There were none. He continued.

"Hekka, I know you've wanted to perform some special research on indigenous tribes. There are a few in Argentina and Chile you might find interesting. Just beware that most died off due to diseases brought by the Europeans after colonization. I don't believe there are many left."

"If they are there, I will find them," Hekka responded.

"And you both need to take the breather I've just ordered, and give these places a visit. Good enough. Hey, you do remember Darryl, right? Does all of our off-the-books travel arrangements out of Nova Scotia?"

They all knew well the mysterious travel man in Nova Scotia called Darryl. He worked wonders with travel arrangements when he wasn't bicycling to every corner of the Canadian Maritimes.

"I've got him on the other line. I'll put you on hold."

Click.

The president turned away and spoke softly. His side of the conversation sounded amicable and agreeable.

Crayle thought having their secure travel plan resource so available seemed somewhat suspicious. But then everything was suspicious in the world of espionage.

Five minutes passed.

The president hung up and turned back to Crayle.

"Okay. You'll fly to Buenos Aires out of Dulles, and catch a boat. A big one. The Royal Princess. It doesn't arrive for a day, so you'll have to visit cemeteries and such."

"Cemeteries? We've been trying to stay out of them."

"Seriously. Darryl says the famous Evita Perón is interred at the one called Ricoleta. That woman, born into poverty, changed the country. Drop by. Pay your respects."

"Having an ultra secret society like Illuminé changing countries is enough."

"Anyway, the first port out will be the one you mentioned."

"Why not just fly there?"

"You can blend in with the huge crowds in Buenos Aires. Not so little Puerto Madryn. Hekka can remain aboard as the ship heads south. She can visit the museums down in the Tierra del Fuego region. Fuegian Indians and all."

"I'd like that."

"Darryl has Mag rejoining the ship due west of Puerto Madryn in Chile. At Puerto Montt, if I recall."

"And Darryl did all this in five minutes?"

"Like I always say. He's good."

"South America seems to be an intersection of what we're both doing. Is there some intrigue here, Kimbel?"

"No intrigue. Allow me to recount. Our favorite travel planning resource, Darryl, has you booked on the Royal Princess out of Buenos Aires. First port drops Magus off at Puerto Madryn—an ages old Welsh settlement not far from your dad's town, Gaiman—and two ports thereafter drops Hekka off at a little burg called Ushuaia. It's at the bottom of Argentina, so you'll both be in the same country. We'll keep track of you both by satellite, and get you back together when you're ready."

"Did you mean to say, when you and Jack Sommers are ready?"

"I'll try to keep the world in one piece during your absence so that isn't necessary."

"There's always a first time."

"Ouch."

"And you're going to watch our baby?"

"Susanna and Luisa will take care of your kid. Perhaps teach her a thing or two. Just until Flori and Marli return from transporting you folks around. She'll be fine."

• • •

The Dassault Falcon 8X departed Dulles and, after a brief refueling stop in Bogota, Columbia, touched down twelve-and-a-half hours after initial departure in Buenos Aires.

Customs was the usual non-entity they'd experienced in their operational travels around the world. That was the least of their worries. The intel they'd received in flight regarding the kamikaze behaviors of the local cab drivers appeared to have been understated, if anything.

Their driver seemed bent on adjusting other drivers' side view mirrors. In between the gasps from the back seat, he did manage to maintain a safe half-inch margin throughout, though, so there was never any actual violence involved. He dropped them off at the port.

Darryl had arranged a pre-boarding tour for them. Their tour bus driver tossed their luggage into the vehicle's storage bin, and they set off at a less threatening pace. The necessary air conditioning and the drone of a tour guide over the sound system put them both to sleep in ten minutes.

After trips to the cemeteries on day one and a full night's sleep at a Hilton, they boarded the cruise ship on day two for their trip south. They remembered the Royal Princess from a previous eventful trip in the Caribbean. The Crayles agreed. No cruise directors named Pattie.

And not only did they know their way around, President Stones, via Darryl, arranged for them to have the best suite on board. Not bad.

CHAPTER 24

The weather in the Republic of Chile was quite nice throughout its late Spring. Especially in the south of central Lakes District. As it always seemed to be in the world of the geopolitical layout, and the attendant and incessant espionage, far more existed to be seen than was readily visible.

The area, ripe with lakes, waterfalls, rivers, remarkable landscapes, and volcanoes, always attracted tourists. The locals included the Hispanic descendents of long-ago pioneers, plus the Mapuche Indian remnants of the indigenous tribes. Another group added small numbers to the mix, but infused a significant cultural variation. Those descended from the original settlers from Germany long ago, plus the more recent escapees of the World War II aftermath. Some of them just wanted freedom and peace. Others, however, wanted much more.

Other than that, there were little more than earthquakes, tsunamis, and volcanic activity to interrupt the otherwise placid existence in modern day Chile.

Wilhelm Rein, along with his just-arrived young adjutant, walked along the streets of Frutillar, Chile. The town had been created on the shores of beautiful Lake Llanquihue by German immigrants centuries before. Unlike the others of Germanic descent in the region, Herr Rein had a steadfast affiliation with a European secret society known as the Aryan Alliance. With some serious forward-moving consequences set in the near future.

"Were you aware, Karl, that Tel Aviv was first settled by Germans? 1871? Now it houses the Mossad headquarters. Those who want us dead."

"We pose no threat to them."

"Not now. But very soon."

"You must tell me how I am to assist."

"In due time. First, you must be *read in,* as the Americans say."

"*Entschuldigung*, uh, excuse me. I am not aware of that term."

"It means you need the information necessary to perform your work. Just enough. Not too much."

"Why?"

"If you are captured and interrogated, you cannot give up more than you know. The big word is compartmentalization."

"I am faithful to the Fatherland and to our cause unto my death. I would not respond to their questions."

Wilhelm Rein considered applying some very special tools he kept under lock and key in order to make his point, but decided against it. "Your answer demonstrates your loyalty. That is good."

"More knowledge then. *Bitte*?"

"English?"

"Please."

"We continue. Adolph Hitler's personal secretary, Martin Bormann, saw to the movement of stock certificates, diamonds, and gold to Argentina before the war's end. The Führer's people saw the so-called writing on the wall, and sent the wealth to a safe place."

"The Argentine government colluded, then."

"We must not use that pejorative term. They cooperated. I continue. Do you know why our political ancestors sent it away?"

Karl, young and inexperienced, gave it a thought. "Of course. The Fourth Reich!"

"*Ausgezeichnet*! Excellent!"

Karl had demonstrated by his body language that he was sincere. Not just kissing up.

"We have utilized much of the hoard just staying alive. And free. The Mossad continues to hunt. Even Shin Bet, the Israeli FBI. But it's always been the Jews. They were blamed for Germany's loss in World War I. Because of the financials. In 1938, the *Kristallnacht* program destroyed Jewish businesses, homes, and places of worship. Not enough. Hitler created *Endlösing*, The Final Solution. To exterminate them."

"I was not aware."

"*Gott verdämmerung*! What do they teach in the schools?"

Karl skipped the rhetorical. "Had the Führer's program been a success, then no post war recriminations, and we would not worry about this now."

"Precisely, Karl. I'm telling you these things, because time will come soon when we must move our Fourth Reich riches."

"Back to Germany?"

Wilhelm Rein smiled his acknowledgment.

"I see. Then the tunnels, underground railway, and these bombs you've acquired play into moving the three kinds of wealth."

"Actually, the gold is what is left. The diamonds were very portable, and we used them first. Then, the stocks."

"I have seen no gold here in the cavern. Where do we keep it?"

"In plain sight, my dear Karl. In plain sight."

Karl reflected on their earlier conversation as they continued to walk about the Germanic town. He recalled the ethnic influences. The *Deutsche Schule*, for instance. He wondered if here at the German School, far from the homeland, the children were taught what they needed to know, when they needed to know it.

"Come, Karl. We stop for lunch."

They enjoyed a pleasant repast at the Club Aleman Frutillar, taking extra care not to make any other than small talk. A meal of tasty breaded pork chops, and beer—one German, and one of the fine artisanal varieties—made for an excellent repast. Rein paid the bill, and headed them back toward their underground lair.

"But I have concerns, Herr Rein. We possess so few bombs. Just the five."

"Ours are very special bombs."

"I want to hear. Please."

"We must herd the Jews to Israel. How we accomplish that I can not yet expose. And then we shall use these weapons. For the second and final phase of the *Entlösing*."

"The Führer shall be pleased at our success, and avenged. God rest his soul."

The young Karl was not too sure of wishing for God to rest Hitler's soul. Nevertheless, he would perform as ordered, and be careful not to challenge his mentor's wisdom.

"You know, young man. We have a history with the atomic weapons that makes using them feel right. Our scientists were spirited from South America to the United States via something called Operation Paperclip."

Rein couldn't know that the word paperclip was rendered in the Finnish language as Hekka. And that he'd meet her someday. Soon.

"Why are we here?"

"So, you wonder how we Germans arrived here? In Chile? The Jews committed their searches for past Nazis to Brazil, Argentina, and Paraguay. And this is a strong country. People. Places. All good. And they left us alone."

CHAPTER 25

The weather was perfect as the Royal Princess cruise ship sailed south from Buenos Aires. Crayle decided to take a break topside as Hekka stowed suitcase contents in their sumptuous stateroom. Having the breeze in his face felt good. It reminded him why dogs always poke their heads out of car windows. His phone rang. The special ring.

The call started in a strange fashion. Via the visual, he could see it was indeed Jack, as the ring indicated, but he seemed to be putting on airs as well as affecting an English accent. Like an aristocrat.

"Pretense, Jack? That's not like you."

"What pretense? I'm having a *cuppa*." He squished down the device's plunger mechanism, dropped in a thimble-full of cream, filled the cup to within a little finger's width from the brim, and took a sip, extending said little finger as he did.

"It seems you've taken a liking to the royalty quest that corrupted Lalumière."

"I've moved up."

"Who says?"

"The president says."

"Playing coy isn't your bag, either." Crayle gestured with his fingers. "C'mon, give it up."

"You recall that the new pope, Alighieri, is helping us out, don't you?"

"Well, I'll be damned! You're running the pope! Holy crap!"

Sommers gazed briefly at his fingernails. "When my clock ticks down to zero, I'm going to Heaven."

"Along with your ex. I'd pay to see that."

"You have to forgive everyone to get in. I'm safe."

"If the pope told you that, he's setting you up."

"Micmac and I have been hitting the cosmos. We ran into a whoop-de-do. Our enigmatic pal, the displaced German, has European roots. Wanna hear?"

No-one used the word 'shoot' any more. "Yeah."

"He's half-brother to the Illuminé Elder. The guy Pattie blew up when she took out Monte Carlo with the mini-nuke.

"Holy crap again!"

"That's two."

"The puzzle pieces are forming up. He's Illuminé, as well. Maybe *Mister* Illuminé in this part of the world."

"And . . ."

"The Elder's removal at Monte Carlo has created a power vacuum."

"Then there are others wanting that top spot, huh?"

"But where?"

"Don't know. Let me know if you come up with anything. I'm still chasing this babe around the northeast. Gotta go."

Click.

• • •

Time passes too quickly. With the incessant meals, thousands of new faces, and plenty of down time with his wife, the sea day respite between Buenos Aires and his destination, Puerto Madryn, Argentina came to an end.

Crayle kissed Hekka goodbye, then *au revoir*, and finally and appropriately, *hasta la vista*. He pulled his suitcase along the gangway to the dock, turned and waved a final farewell.

He hailed a cab. The driver seemed ready to go. With over three thousand passengers coming ashore and needing to go somewhere, he needed to move quickly.

The man seemed a bit disappointed that this passenger wasn't a quick turnaround. He wanted to be dropped off in Gaiman, a ways away. His attitude improved when Crayle handed him the Argentine equivalent of five hundred dollars.

The trip lasted just one hour, the scenery magnificent along the way. The structures appeared as if they would have been more at home across the Atlantic in Wales.

The driver deposited him in front of the police station, and Crayle held up the same amount. "Meet here in three days. Same time."

The cabbie responded to his quizzical look with a nod. And a big smile. Then, he was off. Plenty more fares to be had back in Madryn.

Crayle strolled along. It was if he'd stepped back in time. His father would have walked these same steps. Before coming to the United States. Before marrying. Before joining the Army, being selected for officer candidate school, and being placed in the military intelligence apparatus. Before being sent to Hong Kong as liaison with a Chinese People's Army equivalent. Before being murdered by that man. General Li.

Crayle took no solace in having killed that same General Li in Xian, China not that long ago. It righted a wrong, but didn't bring back his father. A quick shake of his head helped him get back to the present. In more ways than one, he moved on.

But, over there, to his right. He stopped. An interesting Welsh tea house caught his attention. He was unsure why. Then, he extracted his wallet and withdrew the 35mm photographic negative he'd found in his Gone Away box. Those operatives who just disappeared off the grid were unceremoniously characterized as having *gone away*. Working in the CIA's fourth directorate, administration and security, Lenny's father, Sammy, had been charged with collecting Crayle's personal effects. He had later been assassinated at a place called Tysons Corner, Virginia for Illuminé intel he'd lifted from those personal effects.

Crayle held the negative up to the light with the store front to one side. There. There were the Jasmine vines. An exact match. And the rest, exactly as in the negative.

"So, here I have it." He waved the film in the air. "But, why?" he said to himself. "Why was this taken? And when? And why here?"

A few more minutes. A few more questions.

"Did I take this? The camera technology is quite old. Or was it given to me? By whom? Why?"

Curiosity, a necessary trait but often the arch enemy of the intelligence operative, got the best of him. He stepped to the ornately carved mahogany door. It pushed open, giving no resistance.

Darkness. Pitch black. He stepped inside to feel the wall for a light switch. One problem. There was no floor.

Magus Crayle went into free fall. Into a tubular structure that guided him with never ending changes in direction. And faster. Ever faster.

Thirty seconds passed before he struck bottom. Or so he thought. Lights blinked on. He'd landed in a capsule-like entity configured like a World War II fighter canopy.

The cover snapped shut over him. He heard it lock.

He beat it with his fist. To no avail. He heard a whooshing sound outside. He recognized that sound. Below Neuschwanstein Castle in Southern Bavaria.

In that instant, he anticipated the blinding acceleration he'd experienced in Germany. He wasn't disappointed.

The vacuum-enhanced tube permitted encapsulated travel at near 300 miles per hour. The tunnel lights became a blur. It mattered less and less as the cockpit-like transport began to fill with a fine mist.

Crayle held his breath for nearly three minutes before his burning lungs forced him to gasp for breath. For him, the lights went out shortly thereafter.

CHAPTER 26

Hekka Crayle pondered whether there'd been any studies regarding the duration of a kiss. When she parted with her husband at Puerto Madryn, their goodbye kiss might have qualified as a new Guiness World Record. Absolutely no rush. And she missed him right away. Perhaps there was a record for that, as well. Soon it would be evening on the Royal Princess. Darryl had signed her up for Anytime Dining so she could experience new table mates each time.

She wore a black dinner dress and sufficient baubles to be taken seriously. Her life experiences in having a Serrano Indian plus Finnish coloration commonly referenced as butterscotch added intrigue to her natural beauty. It was impolite to stare, especially at a supper table, so men would engage her verbally as they seemed to examine every visible cell. She'd developed an immunity to the extra attention over time. It became her normal.

Off she went to the Symphony Dining Room. Once seated, the standard operating procedure, SOP, was to introduce oneself as briefly as possible. No one would remember names later anyway.

"Hi. I'm Fred Comstock from Calgary, Alberta. Oh, and this is my wife, Carlotta."

"Hi. I'm Charles from Kelowna, British Columbia. Near wine country. Not too far from Kamloops." A moment passed. "Canada? Oh, and this is my wife, Shelby."

Hekka concluded there were only a little over thirty million people in Canada, because the rest were on her cruise ship. Then, she realized that, in late Fall, Canada made its entrance into the Winter weather. Cold and snow. Lots of it. A good reason to be south of the equator where warm Summer was at hand.

"So, Hekka, what do you do?" Fred asked as if it mattered as he examined every aspect of her facial structure.

"I'm a writer. I'm researching a book on this trip. About the indigenous peoples of southern Patagonia."

"Oh," Fred returned. "I always wanted to know that, too."

Charles wasn't going to lose out. "We call them First Nation up in BC. Uh, British Colombia, eh."

"I recognize the abbreviation. My husband and I spent a little time in Victoria." She left out the pitched battle that destroyed Victoria's landmark Craigdarroch Castle and a number of Chin and Li's armed entourage. The warfare, replete with enemy-operated combat helicopters, extended to Beacon Hill Park. "I understand that the numbers of the indigenous were decimated by the diseases of the European explorers. Since they pass down history from generation to generation, I'm hoping to locate modern day survivors."

She noted that Fred and Charles hung on every word. And Shelby and Carlotta were taking mental notes on their men's flirtations. As if the husbands were running a depravity tab. To be paid later.

Hekka spent the following day by the pool. At one point, Fred and Charles spotted her from a partial deck above and nearly hurt themselves rushing down a stairway. She tired quickly of the ensuing testosterone battle, and headed back to her stateroom. She missed Magus even more.

The next port call took Hekka to the Falkland Islands and a grand tour of the East Island. The Royal docked at Stanley, the capitol.

She recalled that her pre-cruise research reflected how two peoples, the British and the Hispanic Argentines, could both worry about who owned the islands, yet ignore that they'd both taken over lands pioneered and occupied by the indigenous tribes.

Frame of reference, she supposed.

The tour took her to the shell of an ages old wooden vessel, to the Historic Dockyard Museum with its replica Victorian Kitchen and 1930's store, past a Hard Rock Café for a touch of modern, and finally to a hillside site topped with a bust of Margaret Thatcher. The guide indicated that Mrs. Thatcher was Britain's Prime Minister during the 1982 war with Argentina. Hekka wondered if the indigenous peoples fought on either side, or stood out of harms way and observed. She intended to find out.

She reboarded prior to the requisite 4 p.m. ALL ABOARD deadline, and proceeded to the top deck.

Whenever cruise ships depart a port, there's always a *Sail Away Party*. With alcohol-fueled drinks in abundance, everyone found an excuse to be cheerful.

Unable to share it with her husband, the experience felt bittersweet. Yet, she knew in her heart of hearts what he was doing was right for him. It was the heritage he knew so little about that would add a connection to his Welsh father and perhaps forge another link between memories restored by the CIA's mind manipulator, Doctor Rorschach.

He needed this in another way. Time to himself. Without Lenny and Alona. Without Micmac. And, painfully, without Phoebe. She realized it meant without herself, as well.

Just a little personal time. She was certain he'd come back refreshed. Come back new.

• • •

At 5 p.m. sharp, the Royal Princess set sail for Cape Horn, and its mystical little island at the southern tip of South America.

It'd been two whole days since she'd seen her husband. She pulled out her phone to call him. But, then, no. Give Magus some space and time, she thought. Then ... reunite later in a major way!

CHAPTER 27

Encapsulated in what appeared to be a WWII fighter canopy, Magus Crayle sped west on his one man bullet train. Unless this underground rail ride was an E-ticket experience add-on arranged by Darryl, Crayle worried he might be captured once more. He thought of not seeing Hekka again, or their new daughter.

To take his mind off worrying what might befall him this time, he retreated into his novelist self. He needed a title for prospective book number three in his spy thriller series. With nothing but granite flashing by all around, his mind achieved true creative freedom. Where to start?

He thought first of his number one nemesis. What of Pattie spiriting Lalumière around the globe to various prisons. When would that end? End the legend of Mitim? Maybe he could call Hekka. Ask her what she thought. No. His cell phone was no good this far underground. Unless they had Wi-Fi. Where to find an idea?

Of course. It was Chin Yao-wu who'd been seduced by absolute power. And the Illuminé had stolen an artifact from the original Ch'in's tomb in Xian to assist. An ancient slab of beautiful crystalline jade had been engraved to provide provenance to the first emperor of China. Sufficient unused space on the jade allowed the Illuminé to forge additional certification, and spread it to modern day Chin.

"Seduced. That's it," he said out loud. He smiled broadly at the creation of his future book title. The Crystal Seduction.

• • •

The capsule blew through the 450 mile breadth of South America's Patagonia region midriff at 300 mph. The vacuum-enabled tube technology cut the transit time to just an hour and a half. The transport vehicle slowed gradually to a stop to keep the impact on humans within doctor-specified limits.

A number of armed men obscured the two-foot wide platform beside his capsule. That started Crayle's jaw down. That each of them sported flat top blond hairdo's with color highlights completed the thought.

"Ferals," he whispered. "Illuminé thugs."

Crayle examined the control panel ahead for a special button. One that would unlatch the canopy. The labeling in German wasn't a help. No levers to the left or right, either. He put on his best plaintive look, a passable French shrug, and waited for some outside assistance.

One of the Ferals pressed his finger on a remote control device.

The lid swung open. A feature popped open the automated six-point safety harness, as well.

The men extracted him from the cockpit, but not in an aggressive, overly rough fashion. They carted him along an access tunnel to a pair of oaken doors, and then through.

"Travelling in those close quarters at that speed, I think I would like to freshen up." Crayle glanced about as if he'd just entered a five-star hotel.

"In due time," came the German-accented response.

Crayle gave an "umph!" as they unceremoniously deposited him into a very old arm chair. And strapped his wrists and ankles, for safety sake. Theirs.

A plump individual sporting a balding head fringed with well-trimmed orange hair and clad in gray Bavarian lederhosen stepped forward.

"Permit me to introduce myself. I am Wilhelm Rein. Aryan principal for all of the Western Hemisphere. Since you speak some German, you should appreciate the name."

"I do speak a little. So, when I wish to summon you, I say, *Komm, Herr Rein*. Same effect if I just say to anyone else, *Komm herein*."

"That is a very funny play on words. Perhaps we shall stick to the English." He nodded agreement with his own proposition, then continued.

"I and my associates…" He made a sweeping gesture toward the Ferals. "… hope you enjoyed your journey, Herr Crayle. On off days, we take turns making the round trip just for the exhilaration."

The spy glanced at them in disbelief. "Right."

"I am sure you could use some fresh air at this point. My men shall prepare you to go out. *Aufwiedersehen*, Herr Crayle."

The Aryan turned and strode out through an individual large wooden door.

CHAPTER 28

Crayle was not sure why it was necessary, but had no choice but to comply with an order from the lead Feral. A couple of minutes later, he stood with his shirt and pants off.

A pair of the Aryan's helpers poked two holes just above each shirtsleeve cuff. Then, two in each pant leg just above the hem. They affixed leather thongs on each wrist and each ankle. Then, directed him to dress again.

With his clothing back in place, they passed the thong ends through the holes. The wrist straps they affixed to his side belt loops. The longer ankle tethers were tied together, affording moderate travel.

"There," one of them said. "We can now take you up top for some fresh air. *Frische Luft* in our native German."

The Ferals escorted him to a basement-like area, and proceeded up a centuries-old stairway. Dark brown hard wood.

After several flights, the leader stepped ahead and unfastened a rope across the stairway's top.

As Crayle passed, he noticed a wooden sign on the cordon.

Authorized Personnel Only.

"Indeed."

They led him past a living room and kitchen replete with chairs, tables, pots, pans, and even a sewing machine that Crayle guessed were from the same bygone era. 1800s, he surmised.

Stepping out the front door was a true delight. Riding inside the minimalist capsule from Gaiman had been like an internal medicine doctor's scope blowing through an intestine at warp speed. A tight squeeze, and too fast to recognize anything. He appreciated the dramatic improvement.

Crayle was thankful to once again, if possibly for the last time, behold green grass and a number of well-foliated trees. Quite a view. He tilted his head up, and breathed the fresh Chilean air deeply.

It felt good. He repeated the process, filling his lungs.

His keepers thought the process quite normal and in order. What they didn't realize was that he was pointing his countenance to the heavens, and saying to himself, "I hope they're watching."

"You partake of the sun, Herr Crayle. Good."

"Vitamins." He didn't add that, when he looked up, and the US spy satellites looked down, there was a microscopic chance that he would be recognized. He'd take those odds versus none at all.

"*Raus*," the lead Feral ordered. "*Zurück gehen*."

"Leave? Go back?"

"Ah, you speak more German than I anticipated. I must update your profile."

They returned as they had come. As they passed the dangling rope with its admonition, and started down the stairs, Crayle didn't feel especially good about being one of the authorized personnel mentioned on the sign.

It seemed the niceties were limited in duration. Back below, he was taken to a different room and lashed again to a chair.

A man walked in he thought he recognized, but didn't. But his attention wandered. He couldn't help but visually examine something off to one side.

"It's Artificial Intelligence, Herr Crayle. Our latest. The Master Race shall become ever superior. We are experimenting with DNA editing. Making the best even better."

Crayle looked over the blond man and woman within two bell jar-shaped glass cylinders, each three feet in diameter and seven feet high.

"I test them when we extricate them from their rest state. I've actually stumped them, but am certain they will evolve to the answer. Would you like to know the question, Herr Crayle?"

The spy gave no reply.

"It is a mathematical enigma of sorts. Known as Xeno's Paradox. Let me see if I can state it in layman's terms. There are two points, A and B. If one starts at A, and in each move covers one-half the remaining distance to B, when, if ever, does one expect to reach B?"

"I believe you're looking at an infinite series solution for that one."

The Aryan's face faded to pale. He turned to the lead Feral. "You must add mathematical sophistication to Herr Crayle's profile."

The Feral noted that this was addition number two in just a matter of minutes. It would seem that the Aryan intel operatives might require some painful genetic restructuring.

The ensuing days would include further trips topside for *Frische Luft*, followed by interrogations. And some very substantive surprises.

CHAPTER 29

Hekka Crayle had been without her husband since dropping him off in Puerto Madryn, Argentina. A daily document, delivered to her stateroom every evening and labeled the Princess Patter, provided activities and lectures, plus a number of eating and relaxation venues. She had time to kill. And, for once, nothing else.

She spent the evening on her private balcony with a book. Given the slight breeze, as well as the absence of Fred and Charles, she drifted off.

• • •

Hekka awoke the following morning to a still otherwise empty bed. In an attempt to partially satiate her insatiable curiosity, she attended one of the numerous informative sessions in the Princess Theater near the bow of the ship. This one provided construction and other details of the giant vessel.

The cruise ship was quite large. Hekka remembered from school the Archimedes Principle. Fill a bathtub to the rim. Climb in naked.

The amount of water displaced and flowing over the sides would match your weight. Weigh the water, you weigh yourself. There were simpler ways like bathroom scales, but how would Archimedes know the Royal Princess weighed 142,714 tons, spanned 1,083 feet from bow to stern, and measured 144 feet in width. Must be some bathtub.

• • •

Hekka Crayle rose bright and early to attend another lecture in the ship's large theater. It provided history to the many mining operations in South America. What most caught her interest were the emeralds. The talk caused her to recall her recent cruise with her husband aboard the Emerald Princess in New Zealand, that she was, herself, a Serrano princess, deserving of an emerald of her own. She wouldn't mention it when she next saw her husband, but half expected that the romantic in him would rise to the occasion and bestow the beautiful gemstone.

In fact, he might be seeking it out at that very moment. Deep underground. In a Patagonian mine. Picking out just the right one. That brought a smile.

Hekka realized self time was important to her, as well. Time to think of her father, but not in the savage way he died at the hands of Sylvain Lalumière's first lieutenant the team knew as TJ. She took a photo album from the blue carry bag supplied by the cruise line. She'd picked a spot protected from the sometimes surprising wind gusts of the southern Atlantic.

Her choice? An adults-only area called The Sanctuary occupied the forward aspect of the top deck, Deck 17. As she sat in the thick padded lounge chair and paged through the album, she noted how young her parents were when they married. One photo showed them sharing lunch at Big Bear's Iron Squirrel restaurant. That look of love followed them to the next page in her mother's native Finland. Hekka recalled too well the Helsinki port-side restaurant where she and Crayle had lunch. Oh, that fateful day.

She'd been kidnapped by the Illuminé and spirited into Germany. To draw Magus into a southern Bavarian trap. In a ruby-encrusted cavern beneath the Disney-like castle at Neuschwanstein.

They had so innocently set out to locate her disappeared mother in her homeland only to discover the trap had been set by arguably the most evil and lethal female on the planet. Pattie Norbrunn. The woman murdered for benefit. She murdered for fun. A simple police blotter would characterize her as a serial killer. Pattie was far from normal. It seemed that every blood-soaked instance Hekka knew about bore out that notion.

• • •

The ship's Patter newsletter labeled the next day a Sea Day, with a rounding of Cape Horn and its tiny islands that night.

• • •

Next came a port at the very bottom of Argentina. Ushuaia. She skipped the usual excursion fare such as a trip to the end of the world, concentrating instead on a museum, Historia Fuegina, for the indigenous tribes of the Tierra del Fuego region.

For a moment, she focused on an ancient canoe, noting the vast difference between that mode of transportation and the luxury and protection of her current ride. The moment was interrupted by a tap on her shoulder.

Before turning, she observed reflections in the large glass cube that protected the canoe. Five individuals stood behind her. Her newly acquired spy sensitivities took over. She was clearly the center of their attention. She reached under her blouse, ready to draw the ten-inch Bowie knife positioned upside down in jungle configuration.

"That won't be necessary," came a female voice.

Hekka turned.

She could tell from their facial structure. All were indigenous.

"A certain individual operating out of Nova Scotia has contacted us. Curious, since we live on an uncharted island with no name."

"That would be Darryl," she said. "He makes my travel arrangements. But, please, take me to your island. We can talk there."

"Take your time here. We have seen it all many times and know the artifacts to be representative of we Fuegian Indians. Meet us in three hours, allowing a half hour for transit, at the *El Fin del Mundo* post office. It means ..."

"I know. I live in Southern California. I speak some Spanish. The End of the World."

Hekka's Smartphone rang. She answered. "Hello, Jack."

"Didn't you drop Mag off at some place called Puerto Madryn? Argentina?"

"I did. Two days after we left Buenos Aires. What's wrong?"

"We're trying out that facial recognition software Micmac came up with. We put in some standard faces and guess what? A satellite picked him up in a Chilean town called Frutillar. I checked your itinerary. You'll arrive there by ship in a couple of days. After Punta Arenas and Puerto Chacabuco. Get off in Puerto Montt."

"Why would he be there?"

"Well, it's probably nothing. Some satellite surveillance system photos come my way from the NGA. Uh, National Geospatial Agency. He looked just fine, but the people standing around him didn't look all that friendly. Maybe that's just because he's a foreigner. You might want to just hop a flight up there on your own. And check it out. Ushuaia has an airport just south of town called Malvinas Argentinas International Airport. I understand the cabbies don't speak English down there, so give them *Aeropuerto Internacional Malvinas Argentinas*. That'll get you done."

"Give me more."

"You'll need to land at the Puerto Montt airport. North of town. Use a taxi there, too. To Frutillar via Puerto Varas. Due north so you won't have to go through Montt. Once there, you'll need to find an outdoor-indoor museum. It shows how some specific immigrants from Europe worked and lived. It's got a name. The German Settlers Museum." Jack provided the street address. And hung up.

She thought for a minute. "Hmmm. I wonder if my new Fuegian friends would like to take a little trip."

CHAPTER 30

The German who characterized himself as Aryan seemed to Crayle to not have enough friends. He just went on and on and on. As if he'd been starved for companionship for several months. What could possibly be next?

Here came the man once again. Returning from a bathroom break, and still clad in his gray Bavarian lederhosen.

"You see, I have friends, Herr Crayle. Some Illuminé, some associates. The latter aid in our quest, they just don't know it. They are ultimately expendable."

"Since I'm neither Illuminé nor Aryan, you're telling me I'm expendable. And you want my assistance?"

"Perhaps I misspoke. When you became my guest, I put that intelligence out on our private network. Who would have thought I would have two major worldwide players respond. Allow me to introduce you to the first. You might just recognize him."

The Aryan tapped on his phone and a door opened. In sauntered a man that Crayle recognized immediately.

"So, the great Vladimir. All the way from Moscow just to have an audience with me. I'm flattered."

Vladimir, who'd never lower himself to seek audience with anyone, turned a bright red.

"Add a little yellow from South American jaundice, and you'd become the old soviet colors."

"The soviet ideal did not die in 1989. Or 1991."

"Not news. Communism hates capitalism—the only way humanity has found to generate the huge amounts of cash your massive social programs require. Socialism and its extreme, Communism. Designed to fail. Wouldn't you agree?"

"An unfortunate oversight by Karl Marx. Without capitalism, we Soviets could either afford to fight America in an overt, confrontational manner, or we could feed our people. Not both."

"Economics 101. Guns or butter. America, a free society, could do guns *and* butter. End game, Vladimir."

"Uh, not quite."

"I know. Anyone who knew the Soviet absolutist system knew that, had Mikhail Gorbachev just hoisted the white flag in surrender to the west, he would have been executed on the spot. But his *Perestroika* wasn't capitulation, was it? As the title suggests, it was a restructuring of the battle lines. Of strategy. To one that you could afford."

"You live up to your genius strategist billing. It seems that the western media trails far behind you in its deductions. Please continue."

Crayle enjoyed his opposition demonstrating arrogance when he was their captive. They would brag and boast. But, more significant, they'd give away their future plans. Every time. He hoped Doctor Rorschach was getting transmissions from the cochlear transceiver planted in his ear canal.

"You stopped chasing the West in military might, and turned your efforts covert. Create mayhem internally in the West, and watch those countries destroy themselves. Costs very little, so your people could eat. And, most important, not revolt."

"The long ago Soviet military threat to the U.S. became unsustainable without a Capitalist money pump as in the West. That's why we went to the General Secretary Gorbachev *Perestroika*—the restructuring. Not to drop Communism and call it quits, but to go covert. Tear down the West from the inside. The only way we could afford. Internally, we even referred to it as Operation Perestroika. We determined what was needed to have the Western democracies eat themselves, and put the plan into action."

"It's taken you thirty years just to get this far."

"This far? We have our professors in your universities. And high schools. We've revived the once-dead racial divide. We've turned a substantial portion of the American population against law enforcement. We've co-opted the Democrat Party and the media. We've … we've … " He began to hyperventilate. "… we control six of seven of your audio-visual media!"

Vladimir slumped into a seat, and grasped the arms.

Crayle probed. "And when you're found out. When I relate your grand scheme to President Stones, and he to the world … "

"You won't leave here alive," the Russian president gasped.

Crayle appeared unrattled by the lethal threat. "We have a phrase in English. House of Cards. You remove one card at the base. They all tumble down."

The Russian smiled his evil smile. "If you connect them with super glue, the 'House' stands forever. I am the super glue. As long as I remain alive, the new House of Vladimir shall stand."

"There was more contained in your covert ploy. Let me see if I can construct the entire list. Please forgive any repetition. Your effort required the following:

1. Revive the racial divide of the 1960's and before.
2. Orchestrate and implement fake protests.
3. Attack financial institutions, especially Wall Street and our stock markets.

4. Compromise political leaders. It would have to be mostly the left since Russia's leaders are still left extremists—communists—in every aspect but name. So, the Democrat Party.
5. Compromise Western university professors. Have them bring extreme leftism into college classrooms. Corrupt the young.
6. Compromise the media. Have them lie and spin the news in your favor. Exclude stories contrary to your party line.
7. Demonize your enemies as racists, nationalists, and sexists.
8. Diminish in status those responsible for defending the peoples of the West: the male of the species.
9. Identify and attack all materially significant opponents. Any new people or commentators that wouldn't fit into the pages of your old propaganda rag, Pravda. Sexual harassment and impropriety charges. You promised women large amounts of extorted payoffs for nothing more than a signature.

And, in so doing, you, dictatorship Russia by another name, didn't even raise a sweat."

"I am impressed. Were you a fly on the wall in our planning sessions?"

"Operation Perestroika was obvious to me. Overt to covert. And given that Russia has produced many chess masters over time, Operation Perestroika became the grandest game of chess in history."

"To be honest, it worked beyond our most imaginative dreams. Upon General Secretary Gorbachev's gambit, America wrote off the Soviet Union and declared victory. The remainder of the West followed. They took the bait whole."

Crayle knew the people believed what they wanted to believe. He resumed listening.

"We piled on. After orchestrating and staging race-divisive and anti-law protests, we moved on to genderism—pitting females against males. We left no stone unturned."

"You were just about to celebrate victory and the demise of Western civilization, giving Marx a major assist in the process."

"Karl Marx forecasted in his book, *Das Kapital*, that capitalism would destroy itself. We just helped it along."

"I do have a question. How did you manage to co-opt previously independent, unbiased news leaders into becoming seditionists and traitors?"

"You should know, Mr. Crayle. The same three ways a spy convinces a citizen of some country to betray it. Money. Ideology. Or an ego-related reason such as revenge."

"You had the three major reasons quite at the ready."

"I use a help word. MIR. Money. Ideology. Revenge."

"You had help from George Orwell on that one. MIR is the Russian word for PEACE."

"So it is. You might be interested to know how we inside the Kremlin referenced those American influencers we turned to our cause." He then listed many names of well-known political and media types, each name prefaced with the honorific, Comrade.

"I notice most of your so-called *comrades* were of the left, but with some key names on the right. I'll remember those names, you know."

"You will die long before you can pass them on."

"Are you going to do the duty?"

"The German will perform the execution."

"And you trust him?"

CHAPTER 31

The day continued on in the underground Aryan lair near Frutillar. As the Chilean Spring drew to a close, the subterranean coolness and dampness asserted themselves.

"I hope the temperature is to your liking, Herr Crayle. If not, I'm sure we can provide a blanket."

The object of his attention sat in an armchair, both wrists and ankles tethered.

The chamber lights clicked off for a second. Then, back on.

Absent a response, the Russian president, having recently declared himself czar and, known solely as Vladimir, announced the arrival of someone new.

"Ah, the signal. I have my own guest. One I am sure you will appreciate."

A guard pushed open the main door.

Crayle turned to a very big surprise. In walked someone he knew of, but had never met. Someone to be pulled down—in CIA parlance—should the opportunity ever arise.

Vlad cast a smile his way.

The man was recognizable due to his recent omnipresence in the media, *Destroy Israel Now* his oft-repeated words. That, and the ruling Iranian clergy were quite well known to the Crayle team and CIA in general. But in this context. No. The Grand Ayatollah striding toward him was, as presented, both Aryan and Illuminé. The connection. The link.

"Good day to you both," the Ayatollah said. "I hope our host has provided you some exquisite Persian cuisine, as well as the heavy Germanic fare."

The German's cheek muscles twitched.

"I'm aware of your long-term link with this man, Vladimir. Are you making some sort of point by bringing Grand Ayatollah Fahsolah, leader of Iran, to South America?"

"You may as well know. When we Russians have reverse-engineered and created our own miniature atomic devices, this gentleman shall be our first customer."

"Yes," said the Ayatollah with a broad smile, "Riyadh, capital of the Sunni infidels, shall be our first nuclear statement to the world. We will quickly supplant the pitiful North Koreans as the mouse that roared the loudest."

Crayle caught something in the man's body language that indicated a different move. A hidden motive. His master strategist self came through as to what that might be. His jaw dropped.

Vlad observed the response. "No, Mr. Crayle. He and I have discussed what you're thinking. I have disallowed an attack on Israel with any of our bombs."

"You trusting each other will put honor among thieves to the ultimate test."

"We're good, as you Americans say. And on a first name basis. You'll appreciate the Ayatollah's strategy, being a supreme strategist yourself." The Russian glanced toward the cleric. "Doreihmi?"

"Thank you, Vladimir. Our first business is to turn the Sunni Arab hordes into proper Shia, as Allah has willed. At that point, we will consider the Israel situation."

"A proper rendering by Russia of the mini-nuclear devices, along with reverse engineered radiation sponges, will leave some regrettable devastation, but a radiation-free environment going forward. Mecca and the Hajj must remain sacrosanct."

"Considering the environment. How contemporary of you. But now you're Czar of Russia. Just as Chin Yao-wu recreated an imperial, emperor-led China after such a long hiatus."

"Emperor, Czar, Führer, Communist General Secretary. All just means to the same end. The same end, Mr. Crayle."

"Power. Total power over the masses by the few. Don't forget that those holding the titles you mentioned, and who held absolute power, ended badly. Chin, Nicholas, Hitler, Stalin. It seems that only karma can reign supreme."

"Enough philosophy, Mr. Crayle. It appears that we are struggling with the bomb-making and the so-called radiation sponge. We know of your recent trip to Hanford, Washington, whence spawned the nuclear technology so critical to us. I, Grand Ayatollah Doreihmi Fahsolah, am here at Herr Rein's invitation to ask, politely at first, for your assistance."

Crayle, Vlad, and Grand Ayatollah Fahsolah were interrupted briefly as a crew drove by in a perpendicular tunnel. The airport-like cart transported what Crayle recognized as one of the Chinese-made mini-nuke warheads. The sort that would sit atop a ballistic missile. Then, four more.

"It's okay that you've seen these. The three of us conferred an hour ago. We decided that you should know every last detail of our plot. Such that you may carry complete knowledge with you."

"To the grave," the Ayatollah added.

Their Aryan host entered via the same set of doors as the others. "Let's not be drastic. Our plan is so foolproof, Mr. Crayle here should be allowed to witness it unfold. And he may rest assured. There are backups for each of us. We will have our way, even if he were to kill us all."

Crayle nodded. "Now there's a thought."

The Aryan motioned. A Feral removed their captive's tethers.

He led the way to a wooden dining table from the Fourteenth Century. They sat as Ferals dressed in white aprons and chef's hats served.

"You should agree to our superiority, Herr Crayle. Our tiny Germanic, or should I say Aryan, community in Europe nearly conquered the civilized world."

"You conquered the French."

"Good point. Quasi-civilized. The food, the drink, and their attempts at bizarre sexual conduct are errant and unnecessary. German fare is of far greater substance. Here, try some of the *kartoffelsalat* that's been placed before you."

"What drugs have you cooked into the German potato salad?"

"Unnecessary. You can't escape our subterranean fortress. You can't be rescued. And, you would be the first to say, there is nothing you know that we need from you. *Ja*?"

It seemed the German was unaware of the multitude of the American spy's previous escapes. And the depth of his new-found knowledge of the radiation sponge.

"Aryan purity, Herr Crayle. We are the top of the enlightened. Of Illuminé. We shall win this time. It is our hour."

"The Aryan race, to which you refer, extends from Germany all the way down to today's Iran. Are the brown-toned Iranians superior, too?"

"A very good question. You are very well informed. Just like the fictional spy. What was his name?"

"Bond… James Bond."

"But we don't deal with fiction here, do we? Allow me to return the conversation to the southern end of our Aryan axis. Dohreihmi?"

The Grand Ayatollah nodded to his host. "By now, you have guessed that I, like the last pope, am a non-believer. You must concede that for the two of us, Zoran—the former Croatian pope—and myself, to achieve the top posts required an unimaginable degree of strategic and tactical planning. Those Illuminé assets responsible possessed intellects matching yours. Wouldn't you agree?"

"Be sure to say a few good words for me when I die. You know. To God. Oh! You can't, can you? You can't even ask for Paradise for yourself. How sad."

Crayle was embedding himself under the faux cleric's skin.

"I will definitely utter a few final words on your behalf." He checked his watch. "In about one hour."

"Listening to him is torture enough. I'll tell you what." Crayle turned to the German. "You need to know about the radiation sponge." Adept at the highest levels in mathematics and science, he launched into an explanation that Einstein himself might have comprehended.

"Perfect, Herr Crayle. I'll set my Smartphone to record. Please repeat."

Before Crayle could restate his previous discourse, the cleric, for the first time, revealed his true self.

The Ayatollah reached up to his neck, and carefully peeled away the rubber likeness. "And you thought this technology was fiction."

Crayle was agasp. The two faces before him appeared as mirror images.

Even Vladimir's jaw dropped. He didn't know that the Iranian and the German were twins. Or clones.

It was the Ayatollah who broke the silence. "*Jawohl, Herr Crayle. Brüder!*"

"Brothers? I feel like I've been here before. Don't tell me that your real names are both Otto."

"*Nein* ... no ... you have killed all of the Ottos. A tremendous loss to our grand cause. No. We are the Wilhelms. Willi for short."

"This is giving *me* the Willies." Crayle shrugged off a chill that invaded his body.

"I appreciate your American sense of humor. Once again, the sponge technicals, and how to defeat it. My bomb gift to the Israelis must render the land habitable—the Muslims need Jerusalem, so please consider outcomes of both with respect to the Aryan goal. It would be an irony that radiation could render the Israeli nuke capability flaccid."

Crayle had more than a little something to get off his chest.

"You, Ayatollah, are in deep trouble. Your great general, Hamid Mohammed, was taken out in Monte Carlo by Pattie Norbrunn. His brother, your top nuclear physicist, Navid Mohammed, offed himself in the suicide aerial attack over Xian, China. Which, by the way, turned the pilot, your last Otto, to paste."

The two men were not taking the recitation of disastrous facts well.

"And the story gets worse. Revolt and poverty mark your regime. President Stones placed new sanctions on your country to prevent nuclear weapons production. His previous new treaty required inspection of military sights. You cannot hold off the Americans president much longer. Perhaps weeks. That is all. Your action has to be drastic. Or else."

The Ayatollah had concocted a scheme. The money in hard, untraceable cash he'd received from a previous treaty had gone partly to terrorist groups as unmarked currency, the rest to the Ayatollah's religious organization headquartered in Switzerland. Two young Swiss women, with French accents from the western region of their country, assisted in the transfer with no questions asked. With the transaction, he joined the other elite criminals of the world with an account in Zurich.

He'd recently told those who protested and rioted against his regime, demanding a secular government, that they must make a mass caravan Hajj to Mecca. Then, and only then, would he transition the governance of the country to them. He also indicated they could even revive the revered old name, Persia, implying a new greatness to match that of the ancient empire.

"Unfortunately, my inventory includes but one flyable nuclear weapon. I intend to blow up Mecca with all the dissidents, find credible means to blame Israel, and then claim to my inflamed and supportive countrymen that those who died in such a deeply religious endeavor would surely be granted an eternity in Paradise. And, that Israel must finally be destroyed."

He didn't know that a second nuclear-tipped missile from the Aryans would also be heading that way.

CHAPTER 32

A new day dawned in Chile's Lakes District, but the American spy held captive there had no way of knowing. He'd wandered into his arch enemy's territory via a seaside Argentine village. A subterranean rail system had transported him west across the continent to the Chilean coast. Now, strapped to an arm chair in the underground replica of a Fourteenth Century German home, the future looked particularly grim.

"Good morning, Herr Crayle. You slept well, I presume."

"The handcuffs and windowless cell provided a complete sense of security." Crayle glanced about. "Where are your friends?"

"Oh, the Russian president and the Iranian leader had a plane to catch. Taking their newly acquired mini-nuke bombs home."

"I know this sounds a little harsh, but you bastard! They'll kill innocent people by the tens or hundreds of thousands!"

"No, no, Herr Crayle. With one apiece, they will have to deploy them strategically."

"And pretend they have more?"

"Precisely. Not to worry. I still have three of my own. And a lifetime supplier in the Orient."

Crayle knew the supply and supplier of the miniaturized nuclear devices had dried up. He'd seen to it personally while in Hong Kong. But he thought better of giving up the intel until it would produce the optimum effect. "You can't kill your way to the top. The rest of the world will stop you."

"We shall see. Now, I'd like to introduce someone you won't recognize."

Through the doors strode a man in clerical garb.

"May I introduce Nuncio Hernandez. The pope's representative to Chile. He resides just north in the capitol, Santiago. I'll leave you to chat. It seems my shipment of Oktoberfest beer has just arrived. I must sample it." He left.

There was something about the Nuncio that was immediately unlikeable.

"Señor Crayle. I've heard of you from the previous pope."

"I met Zoran myself. In his native Croatia. It's a shame how he died in Monte Carlo. Up in smoke, you could say." He paused for the sarcasm to sink in. "I'm guessing, because you are here with the German, that you are, like him, Illuminé. Like him and the previous pope, an atheist."

"Well done, Señor Crayle. And like the other two men, I am here to receive my very own mini-nuke."

"So, what is it, Nuncio Hernandez? Blow up the Vatican?"

"Perhaps Jerusalem. The Germans have hated the Jews for a long time. I can curry favor with the Aryan."

"I see. Willi wants that in exchange. What do you get out of flattening religion's most holy city?"

The nuncio laughed. "Señor Crayle. You have a persistent habit of living, and escaping. I'll keep my scheme to myself. For now."

The German returned toting a pair of Oktoberfest six packs. And a straw for his wrist-bound prisoner. "This was a fine year. Drink up, gentlemen."

Crayle in *oh, well* mode tried the beer. With quality standards in effect since the 1500's, he concluded that the Bavarians couldn't produce a bad batch of beer.

After the trio downed two bottles apiece, the German stood. "Well, Nuncio, I'm afraid it's time for your departure. Your bomb has been loaded. Please, follow me to the vacuum tunnel transport to Puerto Madryn." He turned to Crayle. "As with the other two, he will fly by private jet from Argentina's east side. Far from our place of operations here in Chile. We always fly in and out of that airport. To do so from here would attract unwanted attention. Don't you agree?" he asked.

Crayle didn't answer. His beer had been adulterated with a sleeping potion. He slept.

CHAPTER 33

Hekka felt there was no time to waste. She and the five best Fuegino braves flew from Punta Arenas in the far south into El Tepual International Airport on the outskirts of Puerto Montt, also in Chile. The Lakes District.

They took a cab north just under nineteen miles to Puerto Varas. The 20,000 Chilean Peso fare caused a near heart attack. The cabbie's verbal defibrillator surprised the American. He asserted a willingness to accept American money which, he tapped on his Smartphone, translated to $28.65. Hekka paid him plus tip, and they were off.

Quite by accident, the sextet stumbled on a boat rental place. She viewed it as a sign from above. There in the water not thirty feet from them, three canoes. The Fuegian braves checked them out. They seemed unsure about the man-made hulls of the watercrafts, but Hekka assured them they'd be fine.

"The canoes are natural," she said. "Anyone watching would never expect a water borne assault squad."

"They do not appear natural."

"Crafted from the fiberglass tree." She watched as they scanned the periphery for the requisite forest. "Far from here," she informed them. Clearly they'd seen nothing similar on Tierra del Fuego Island.

She paid, and they paddled off on the beautiful large Lake Llanquihue. North. Toward the other lakeside Germanic village, Frutillar.

They made landfall.

• • •

"I believe I'll have to abandon you here, Herr Crayle. Come along, please." The German uncuffed Crayle and pulled him along to a rocket sled. One with a mini-nuke attached. "As the tunnel from Gaiman does, this tunnel to Volcán Osorno zigs and zags. The theory is that when this sled reaches the natural wall beneath and explodes, the back force will disseminate due to the switchbacks. Very little will reach this place. The detonation will activate the volcano and send streams of lava headed for the capitol, Santiago. Hearing and feeling the explosion, people will run for their lives. My people will rescue the gold from the museum and be away before the lava arrives. It will, of course, turn the museum and its environs into molten metal and glass. There will be no evidence left for the authorities."

"If it works, the insurance companies will pay the museum owners and you'll be off somewhere with your riches."

The man who considered himself an Aryan genius acknowledged with a nod Crayle's recognition of a brilliant plan. "There's more, Herr Crayle. Utilize that exceptional mind of yours."

"Of course! You own the museum. The insurance payoff will double your take."

"They say, *greed is good.* I say, *more greed is better.*"

"Triggering a volcanic eruption for excessive personal gain won't win you any humanitarian or environmental awards."

The other man took a step back. "Speaking with you has been an honor. But now, I must send you on your way. Half an hour should be plenty of time for us to escape." He set the bomb timer to thirty minutes and pressed the control button.

The sole sound, a timer ticking.

The next instant violated that tranquility.

CHAPTER 34

The heavy oak doors leading to the stairs and the big house above burst open.

Hekka and her five Fuegian friends charged into the room. She pulled a .40 SIG Sauer pistol from her purse. The Indians had their bows and arrows ready to rock.

The German pulled a WWII 9mm Luger sidearm to hold them off. He stabbed at a red button with his free hand. He signaled from his phone.

Seconds later, five Ferals sporting Heckler and Koch MP5 submachine guns poured in through the door.

Seeing a fusillade coming, Hekka and the Indians ducked behind a substantive old walnut dinner table, tipping it over toward the Germans.

With weapons firing on full automatic, the gunmen swept the area facing their leader. They could hear him moan as they obliterated priceless artifacts.

Being orderly, prototypical Germans, they all started to fire at the same instant, and ran out of ammunition likewise. They began the three-second reloading process.

Like a whack-a-mole game gone berserk, the Fuegians popped up one at a time. They loosed their wooden arrows.

Thunk!

Thunk!

Thunk!

Thunk!

Thunk!

Having brought bows and arrows to a machine gun fight, they couldn't afford to miss. They didn't.

Five hits.

Five hearts.

Five Ferals down.

Hard.

Since his Feral personal guard always had his back in the past, Wilhelm Rein carried no extra magazines. Out of bullets, he sprinted for the door. To escape.

What sounded like a helicopter blade at full spin was in reality Hekka's Bowie, thrown with all her strength. It slammed, point first, into the German's shoulder. Then, the second volley of five indigenous arrows perforated him.

In his 1880's garments and now affixed to the period oak door, he appeared to be a gruesome adornment. And he wasn't dead.

Hekka ran to see if he posed a threat. He did not. She pried her Bowie from his body.

Still fastened to the volcano-destined rocket sled, Crayle called for their attention. "Bomb on timer! Get his key! Get me off this thing!"

They did. Hekka raced over and cut loose her husband's bonds.

He resisted as she tried to pull him away.

"Wait! His computer."

Crayle ran to the German's desk and flipped open the laptop.

"It requires a password. I'll try... Hitler. No. Aryan. No. How about Superior Race?" He pressed ***Enter***. Waited a second. "That's it!"

His eyes poured over the icon-full screen.

"Magus!" Hekka tore at his arm. "The bomb?"

"Just a second."

He touched an icon depicting the Russian. Then, chose ***BOMB***.

Just one item popped up. ***DESTRUCT***. He touched it.

COMMUNICATIONS FAILURE.

Back to the initial screen.

"Magus!"

"I have a chance to save a whole lot of people. Next I choose... Ayatollah."

He touched ***DESTRUCT***.

COMMUNICATIONS FAILURE.

"Magus, please. You've tried. Let's get out of here!"

"One more. The Nuncio."

DESTRUCT.

• • •

Far out over the Atlantic Ocean on its way to the Vatican, one of the Roman Catholic country's jets suddenly went nuclear. The news went out to the world. Those who'd been around, or had worked for, the Nuncio to Chile considered it a miracle.

• • •

Back in the caverns beneath Frutillar, Crayle was done. No time to go back and try again for Vladimir or the Ayatollah.

He led them to the vacuum transport system, with which he was quite familiar. He remembered well that first day.

Crayle quickly explained to Hekka how the modules operated. He was surprised when she repeated his directions to the Fuegians in their indigenous language.

They quickly linked enough together to spirit them all away. Toward Gaiman in Argentina, Puerto Madryn, and flights out. Away from the bomb.

At 300 miles per hour, the eclectic team was well away when the clock ticked down. To zero.

The timer was deadly accurate. Precisely thirty minutes after the German had set it, the bomb ignited.

Pointed away from the escape tunnel to spare the temporarily augmented Crayle team.

Far enough from civilization to kill no one.

And producing seismic activity at that distance inadequate to activate Volcán Osorno. And the chain north to Santiago.

CHAPTER 35

The Grand Ayatollah and the self-proclaimed Russian czar, Vladimir, arrived in Tehran. The latter preferred to continue on to Moscow, but succumbed instead to the hospitality offered.

He understood. His deep ties with Syria and Iran had a political component. He also knew that the Middle Eastern women with their big eyed beauty could resolve his insatiable lust on each trip.

The Ayatollah assigned a name to his first deliverable nuclear device, the one he intended to target Mecca. On the side, he had painted the word, ARMAGEDDON. He addressed this to Vladimir, indicating how he intended to create an Armageddon of biblical proportions, send millions of devout Muslims to Paradise, and initiate the destruction of Israel, America, and the West in the process. Prior to the big event, he planned to execute a monster of an event. A mass cleansing. Of the pilgrims. Of the warriors.

The Ayatollah observed the Samovar set before them by his servant, who passed out two cups. "I understand from my information bureau . . ." He referred to Iran's spy agency, MOIS. ". . . that you take your hot liquids very hot. I take mine a bit tepid, if I may say."

Vlad took a sip of the steaming liquid, careful not to scorch his lips. "Your intelligence is quite accurate. Since I take my drink in private, no one should know. I shall have a word with my adjutant, Raspi."

The Iranian knew well of Vlad's lieutenant called Raspi and his descendency from the 'mad monk' of long ago, Rasputin, of czarist times.

The Russian took another sip. "Because of our long-standing relationship, I know you want to share a 'grand tactic' with me. That's the term your emissary used."

"You are aware from the words I spoke in South America, that my grand strategy is to destroy Israel, but leave the land inhabitable. You must also know from the public discourse that the American president, Stones, has given Israelis new anti-missile technology with a 100% success record. Therefore, no missiles we can send will ever reach apogee let alone land fall or air burst effectiveness due to these systems."

"I am aware. The same systems render my own missiles … flaccid, shall we say." He took another sip of the tea. "My, this is especially tasty. What is it?"

"A special and very secret blend. But, I continue my story. We cannot smuggle nuclear devices into Israel, because of its first class air traffic and port controls. And past that confounding wall."

"You cannot destroy them from within then, either. Bribes, ideology, and ego-related motives such as revenge are all precluded by the Mossad and the Shin Bet. I sense there is something else. Something innovative. I'm dying to know. Please … "

"As you are dying to know, I am needing to tell. You are, by now, aware of the Hajj. Those with the financial means and physical nature necessary for the six day journey are expected to make it at least once in their lifetime. Without it, well, that is up to the Creator." The Iranian leader smiled as he delivered his punch line. "And if Israel were to destroy Mecca?"

This one caught Vladimir by surprise. He took a long gulp of the still hot liquid. "My God! But … there's no way you could …"

The Ayatollah smiled. "No way?"

"They have the missiles. They have nuclear warheads. If you could somehow hack the command and control system, cause a launch, and direct the missile to Mecca, the entire Muslim world would erupt."

"The classic weapons to which you refer do not benefit from the radiation sponge invented by the Chinese. Mecca and surrounds would be uninhabitable forever!"

Vlad glowed red. "And if you cannot cause a nuclear missile launch from Israel and target Mecca, what is your Plan B? You recall," he scolded. "I told you before. You must always have a Plan B."

"And I do have a Plan B. If nothing else, I am a furtive listener."

"I can't wait." He finished the cup, and pushed it forward. "This is delicious. I must have more."

"That won't be necessary."

"What?"

"Remember the traitorous Russian agents who defected to the West? The ones you killed with the radioactive agent, Polonium 210? Novichok?"

"Those were only rumors planted by the West. But, yes, I remember."

"And the symptoms?"

"Of course. It was I who discovered—created, if you wish—this lethal weapon during my tenure at the KGB. First, there is a flushing and reddening of the face. And then …"

"The trembling."

Vlad grabbed the Ayatollah's cup. Full!

Iran's top cleric and leader leaned in as Russia's new czar-elect fell back in his seat. Then, onto the floor.

"Your agenda, the Russia-first agenda, had to come to an end. We shall no longer retain the former relationship."

The Russian gasped, and struggled to speak.

"If anything happens to me, the czarina becomes the ruler of Russia. She will have a great revenge. Against you. Against Iran."

"She and I have spoken."

The Russian's red face blanched.

"More than that, actually. Her agenda was always to become sole monarch. The only question she had, was how to rid herself of you."

Vlad continued gasping. "But how? The tea?"

"She told me you carry a vial of Polonium in your pocket. Just in case."

With difficulty, Vlad extracted the vial. He couldn't see the liquid for the nano-engineered coating of the radiation sponge material from the Chinese. With his failing strength, he shook the vessel.

Empty.

"By the way, she was quite good in bed."

Vladimir couldn't believe his ears. He'd been so sure he owned the czarina sexually. "How did I let my guard down?"

"You kept your vial of nerve agent in the nightstand at the Aryan site in Chile, didn't you?"

"Yes, but how ..."

"Ways, my friend, Vladimir. Ways. No one observed the person slipping into each of the rooms, holding a new edition of the Gideon Bible. Replacing the old with the new."

"I saw no one."

The Ayatollah produced a devilish grin. "Perhaps she knew you were in the bathroom. Demonstrating your ambidexterity in pleasuring yourself."

Vlad lay there, nonplussed. He'd rested assured that his was the best counter intelligence agency in the world. "It was Crayle!"

"Not this time. You didn't see her before? The nun?"

"What nun? Nuns don't place Gideon ..." A hundred pound sack of pre-vodka potatoes crashing down on his head could not have had greater impact.

"*The rogue American! Her! Pattie!*"

"I slept with her, too, by the way. As schooled and good at assassinations as she is, the danger made the sex even better."

"You're a man of the cloth. You—"

"There are times, my dear Vlad, when the sins of the flesh and the sins of the cloth align. Coincide, one might say."

In the ensuing seconds, Vlad settled his head on the cold floor.

And expired.

The Grand Ayatollah took a moment to address the corpse. "I shall blame the Mossad Kidon. I will provide proof of death such as a severed finger, but no body. Plan B could be modified to send Iran missiles toward Israel in retaliation for killing Vlad on Iranian soil. Place his body in with the warhead to dispose of it. An 8,000 degrees Fahrenheit explosion would do the trick. The Russian people would rally around the czarina against Israel and all Jews. The Ayatollah noted that total control over a people, his people, required an *evilized* enemy. Hitler knew that. Stalin knew that. It always seemed that the Jews were the default culprits.

CHAPTER 36

It had been a long journey from South America. First the bullet train across Patagonia. The flight from Puerto Madryn to Tehran, having to listen to the great Vladimir the entire distance. The potential challenges with the new czar of Russia became, upon his death, in the rear view mirror.

Finally at ease, the Grand Ayatollah descended from ground level and stepped into his most private quarters, an exact replica of the Roman Forum. Only in his palace. No one else was allowed in these spaces. Under any circumstance. Retreating here brought him a supreme form of peace.

He recalled how he had read about and had come to feel Julius Caesar in his bones early in life. Even before his religious commitment. And abandonment thereof. He wondered. If Caesar were alive, would he have approved of the idea to send a nuclear-tipped missile to Mecca? The great Roman emperor, Caesar, having been a practicing Roman Catholic, might have entertained the thought. But an ayatollah? A grand ayatollah? Himself?

One deep breath latter, he glanced around to appreciate the adornments he'd acquired. The short sword wielded in combat by the great Roman general. The period draperies. The original artifacts. All set the mood. But most of all it was his prized possession—the life size, self-aggrandizing bust commissioned by the great Caesar himself.

He heard a rustle behind and turned. There, for the first time ever, his colleagues, the other four grand ayatollahs, had somehow infringed on Grand Ayatollah Doreihmi Fahsolah's exclusive personal domain.

He'd been away. His trip had been a success. Did the lesser visionaries come to congratulate him on his genius plan, or to console him on its likely failure due to circumstances beyond his control?

They approached across the Italian marble floor, the only sound the rustle of their formal religious attire as they did.

At a distance of three feet, they halted.

The one who was his second in the line of succession raised his hand in a Roman soldier's stiff-arm salute. He spoke in a most solemn voice.

"Hail, Caesar."

The Grand Ayatollah began a smile.

The auspicious visitor continued. "We convened to contemplate your plan to attack the Jewish state with newly acquired nuclear warhead on one of our ICBMs. We were emotionally attracted to the idea, but the Jews will respond in kind. We have but the one device, as you have confided. We felt it necessary to confer with you before any irreversible action was taken."

The leader's smile widened.

"I shared the notion before to this purpose. That you would consider it, and either buy in, as the Americans say, or not. Not to worry. I have forged a much better plan."

The relief in the others was immediately evident.

"If you will allow me…"

They nodded in unison.

"Not Haifa. Not Tel Aviv. Not Jerusalem." He paused for effect. "Not Israel."

"You could have told us. Saved us the consternation."

"Out of necessity, I didn't share the new target with you before my trip to South America." He paused for effect. "Mecca."

"*What!*" they cried out in unison. "You are insane. Destroy the ability of those physically and financially able to make the journey? *The mustati*? Six days of holy commitment? The seven treks counterclockwise around the central Kaaba? To engage the sacred Black Stone? All destroyed for eternity?"

"But think of the benefit. Muslims throughout the globe will be obligated to make the journey, not to Mecca, but to the Israeli land. To destroy every one of our enemies there. I will then declare an end to Israel, and the reinstatement of that country's original intent. The Holy Land. What do you say to that?"

They encircled the Grand Ayatollah, leader of Iran.

Then, slowly moved in.

His countenance turned ashen. Depleted. "You men must have intimated at every step, save the details, of my intent ... from the outset. Of my plan to attack Mecca. And blame the Jews."

The other four drew the traditional and, at this moment, requisite items of apparel, Muslim daggers, from their waist bands.

No one said a word. Not even his second-in-command and longtime friend.

The only words spoken, as they plunged their razor-sharp knives into the chief cleric and Iranian leader, were his.

"*Et tu, Hakim?*"

CHAPTER 37

Darryl, who performed the travel planning functions for the CIA's off-the-books Strategic Situations Office, sat in his hillside abode overlooking Nova Scotia's Cape Breton Island municipality known as Glace Bay. His guests would arrive soon at the Sidney airport some twenty miles distant. He'd already obtained the necessary and freshly manufactured passports from the Canadian Security Intelligence Service, the spy agency informally known as CSIS. It proved a lot easier for Americans to travel in that manor than with their own valid documents. It meant no questions asked.

He remembered in vivid terms the last scramble he'd had with this team. A direct call from Jack Sommers informed him that the Crayle team was on its way. Shortly. He was to have all ID's and passports ready in fake names and set up for a cabin on the Queen Mary 2. It was to be a five exclamation point operation. Then there were the weapons for them. And coordination with a Special Air Services team from Britain. A lot like shuffling a deck of cards and randomly drawing five with millions of lives hanging in the balance. He almost forgot. And get them on a helicopter to be dropped onto the ship.

Darryl knew he needed to get the Crayle team to Paris for the forthcoming coronation on Christmas Eve. French non-government leaders still stood in for the formal leaders killed not long ago in Xian, China. In the nuclear air burst that also took the life of the new emperor, Chin Yao-wu. They needed a new head of state and a legitimate governing body going into the new year. It had become his role to get the team from the United States via Canada to Paris in time for the big event. To ensure that it went off as scheduled.

Wow! France was going monarchy. He wondered, was it just to poke its ages long adversary—the one across the La Manche channel with its constitutional monarchy—in the eye? Not Darryl's problem. And he'd learned long ago not to try and solve problems that weren't his.

At times like these, he had second thoughts about his career choice. He'd spend a good part of the year in Southern California where the number of cycling days approximately equaled the total number of days. Then, back to Nova Scotia for timely efforts on behalf of the CIA. All with the blessings of the CSIS.

Oh, well. Back to work.

He planned to park their recognizable Dassault Falcon 7X jet in a hangar. They'd transfer to a brand new, Canadian-manufactured, Bombardier Challenger 650. With the Canadian passports, the travel would be easy. And non-stop.

He mused whether those like himself, who risked their lives for God and country, would ever receive their just rewards. Recognition? A national medal? He knew that leader Crayle was in with the American president. Perhaps the country's highest civilian honor. The Medal of Freedom.

Darryl, quite adept with computers, could then jury rig the text of the medal replacing United States of America with the Dominion of Canada.

He shook his head. "No."

When they were on their way, he'd pile his favorite bike in the back of his car, and head off to catch the ferry at Caribou. He'd purchase a round trip ticket for $20 Canadian and head to the little burg called Wood Islands. On Prince Edward Island. From there, he'd hop on his two-wheeled transportation and perform his constitutional trek on Highways 1, 4, and 16. That would put him back to normal. Until next time.

CHAPTER 38

For two very rough years, the people of France sought redress. No one could recall their countrymen ever dumpster diving just for a little food. They had literally run those in governance out of town after a small nuclear explosion in a northern suburb of Marseille. And that apparently premature detonation had been set off by Muslim immigrants with a plan to destroy that or some other French city. "Hungry and unsafe," they chanted.

In apposition, the Legend of Mitim had made the rounds once more. He had been seen and heard while wearing the iron mask, placed upon him by his suppressors. His rightful ascendance to the throne denied. None of them actually saw the man without the mask, and none of them knew him as Sylvain Lalumière.

The rumors now spread that the man himself, exiled to all of the infamous prisons of the other Man In The Iron Mask, would arrive in Paris in short order. Although he'd not spent a single day righting the wrongs of the country, he nevertheless remained their unrelenting hero.

Citizens travelled from every region of the country, from the rest of Europe, the United States, Africa, and Asia. There was barely standing room on the city streets. And then there was the press. The once despised Yellow Journalism of the past had become mainstream. Every quasi-news agency tried to outdo the others in the brightness of the yellow, and, too, its darkness. One report speculated that Napoleon did not die, but rather had been frozen in the Arctic. Surely this Mitim was him brought back to life. It made no matter that Napoleon was more than a foot shorter than the masked man based on actual sightings.

Only one question remained. Would he possess the Black Diamond, which was the key to the monarchy?

CHAPTER 39

After a quick stop at Dulles Airport for fuel and babies, Flori Sommers collected the Lipschitz pair and Micmac. The Crayles much longer trip to Nova Scotia's Cape Breton Island landed at the same airport in the province's primary northern city, Sydney.

The off-the-books spy-trip logistics expert, Darryl, met them on the tarmac. As they deplaned, Crayle noticed that the man arrived on a high end bicycle. He glanced about.

"You intend to haul five adults and three babies plus our luggage around on that? I admire your optimism, but…"

Darryl nodded at a hangar just fifty feet ahead of the jet. As if on cue, its large door rolled open. "It's a double wide. Have your pilot pull in next to the Bombardier. We'll transfer the luggage and then you're off again. Non-stop to Paris Orly."

Crayle strode to him. "No pomp and circumstance for us, huh? Trying to get us off Canadian soil ASAP?"

"Before you Yanks cause any trouble. Any more trouble, eh."

"We'd like to freshen up a bit. Hekka and I started the day in Frutillar, Chile. It's been a long ride. You have laundromats here?"

"Washer and dryer aboard your new ride. Ultra comfortable beds with those new pillows you see on TV. I figured you need to get to Paris, plop into your favorite hotel, zero out the jet lag, and be fresh for whatever op you've planned."

"Favorite hotel?"

"Yes. I've booked you into the Hôtel Saint Louis en l'Isle. It's on Île Saint Louis. Remember? Next to Île Notre Dame? The one with the cathedral? It's the same one you worked out of when that Sylvain Lalumière and his wife tried to plant a mini-nuke high in the Eiffel Tower. And blow the place up."

Crayle remembered the night in the most vivid terms.

New Year's Eve.

The French government gathered in the plaza below.

Thunder, lightning, and torrential rain blew in from the west.

Tower-borne mega fireworks at midnight.

Yes, he remembered.

CHAPTER 40

The petite woman shook the tall man on the bed with extreme vigor. He'd been out for most of the past twelve hours. As he roused, he peered about, and noted his all too familiar surroundings.

"We're going, Sylvain," she said, exited. "At long last, we're going."

"Where am I? What is this new prison? Are we still in Australia?"

"No, you silly goose. We're in South America."

"Where?"

"The southernmost tip."

"I suppose it's not like this is the end of the world."

"Oh, but it is. They call it *El Fin del Mundo* in Spanish. The End of the World."

"Then I'm going to die."

"*Non. Non. Non,*" she responded in French.

"I'm in prison. Again." He walked over and pulled at the rusted bars. They didn't budge.

"My darling Sylvain. I brought you out of Australia before those three nuclear bombs went off. I saved your life." She gave him a moment to realize the gravity of what she'd accomplished. "The Europeans created this wonderful prison years ago. For their worst criminals."

"I hardly qualify."

"True. But, as I said before I was interrupted, we're going home!" She planted a heavy kiss on his lips. "It's our time, Sylvain. We're going to France!"

That got his attention. "When?"

"Today."

"Wait. What about that Magus Crayle … and his team? Please tell me that they finally perished in the Australian explosions. As they were supposed to do."

"Not exactly. He's being held just north of here. By one of those Aryan types. He, Willi, promised he would see to it."

"Three nuclear bombs couldn't kill him!"

"Rest easy, my love." She unlocked the cell door. "We go to Paris. To our coronation in two days. With just one stop along the way."

"Stop? What? Fuel?"

"Uh, no."

"Where?"

"Devil's Island."

• • •

Lalumière next awoke in yet another prison. But this one closer to home. Closer to his culture.

"They call it Devil's Island. Northeast coast of South America. Just offshore from, wait for it, French Guiana."

"That it is French should make me feel good. I know of this place. Most prisoners died here. And I know that the Man In The Iron Mask, my namesake, never was interned here. So …"

"This is our last stop. Before returning home. Freshen up. I have a boat waiting to take us to Cayenne, the capitol. From there, a flight to Paris. What do you think?"

"Can I trust you this time?"

"You can trust me anytime. May not work out. But you can trust me."

• • •

When he'd dressed, they made the trek to the boat. Not the type of prisoner ship of old, but a brand new James Bond kind of boat. Fast. Comfortable. And with a fully stocked bar.

"Did you know they had their very own Sylvain here?"

"Other than me?"

"He was one of few who escaped."

"That is good."

"Uh, I'm afraid that was the extent of the good news. He stepped in some quicksand. But we'll avoid that like all the other impediments to our rise to power. *Vive la France, mon amour!*"

"*Eh, oui. Vive la France.*"

CHAPTER 41

By now, the entire world had been apprized of the upcoming coronation in Paris, France. It surprised some of the political pundits that what had become the lore and legend of the modern day Man In The Iron Mask had seeped into the global public consciousness.

T-shirts, wedding sets of china, coffee mugs, and assorted other print-enabled media bore the likenesses of the prospective king and queen. The Legend Of Mitim biography, suitably embellished, became available in print and all eBook types in forty-seven languages.

None of the aforementioned pundits could remember the last time a democracy transformed to a monarchy. But everyone jumped on board. It was exciting in a positive way. No more electing representatives who didn't represent, they thought.

The consequence of the unusual and huge influx of well-wishers and gawkers arriving by planes, trains, and automobiles jammed the roadways. Logistical plans fell by the wayside.

Relic properties like the Tuilleries were transformed into hostels to handle the overflow of people.

All those in charge of anything realized the same problems would reverse themselves after the festivities when everyone headed back out. Returning to Africa, India, Russia, the entire Western Hemisphere, and so forth.

And there was more. Security for such an event had no modern precedent. The local forces, augmented by on-loan forces from across the country, did everything in their power lest the happening be besmirched by violence.

Fire brigades readied against all odds of being able to respond to an alarm.

But it seemed all to the good. No more election manipulations. The French people took the *ordained by God* notion to heart.

This was their time. The time the great Mitim would unmask himself to the people, and be their king.

CHAPTER 42

Everyone in the flight path knew who rode in the state-owned airliner that passed overhead. News across the globe reported the head of the country known as the Great Bear would be attending the coronation. They didn't know whether to cringe, or to appreciate the arrival of such a global dignitary. One of the most important. Perhaps, second to the American president. What was said inside the jet, however, stayed on the jet. Security stood at its highest level.

"We all converge on the City of Light," Anastasia Romanov, Czarina of Russia, opined as she gazed out over Paris. "So ironic. Light as in enlightenment. The core of the Illuminé belief system."

It was amazing how seamlessly the czarina's new trusted aide moved from the recently deceased new czar, Vladimir, to her. Raspi furrowed his brow. "Who's invited?"

"The one with the Swedish queen. Jean-Marc Lalumière. With the coronation, his father, Sylvain, achieves the title, King of France. Number One. At that very moment, his son becomes Crown Prince of France—Number Two. On the other hand, if the son marries the queen of Sweden, he becomes King of Sweden. Some choice."

"The pope will attend the coronation. Does that make him Number Three in the secret organization?"

Anastasia shook her head. "He's not like the previous pope. This one's not Illuminé."

"So he's not an atheist? Not like us?"

"No, Raspi. I'm afraid he's a real pope. I will be Number Three of the Illuminé attending. Sweden, France, and Russia. We shall represent the future of Europe."

In his reverie that followed, she lost even the presence of her most intimate advisor.

"General Secretary Gorbachev was most prescient in a phonetic sort of way. *Perestroika.* The restructuring has become the Paris Troika."

"It is said that good things always come in threes."

• • •

It would have been normal for the Queen of Sweden and her consort, Jean-Marc Lalumière, to fly in the royal aircraft to Paris for a coronation. They'd do all the proper things according to protocol, and then fly back in time for supper.

Jean-Marc was awakened unceremoniously by the queen shaking him and telling him they needed to be at the royal dock by 7 a.m.

He twisted to check the bedside clock. Six. He checked again. It still said six. "The coronation is tomorrow," he whined.

"We have special transportation. When the coronation is complete, and you've officially become Crown Prince of France and its territories, you will need to know the value of pomp and circumstance."

"I already know the value of uninterrupted sleep."

"Come. Come. Come."

She pulled him toward the bathroom. "Put those on. After you shower, of course. You smell."

"Smell. Like what?"

"You know well like what."

The royal limousine did manage to get them to the dock on time, even though their route had been leaked and well wishers tended to impede progress.

Jean-Marc now understood what the queen had meant by pomp and circumstance.

There in the water, dockside, floated one magnificent ship.

"It is called the Vasa. It has been renovated to rigid modern reconstruction standards."

"I've heard of this vessel. It was built for combat when your country fought against a Poland-Lithuania alliance."

"Very good."

"And it was built to your king's specification, and sailed for the first time in the 1600s. Am I right?"

"Yes, you are. Befitting, it shall transport us to Le Havre and up the Seine to Paris. For our royal arrival."

"Uh. As I remember, its first sailing lasted just a few minutes. A gust of wind came up, caused it to list to port, and sea water poured in through its gun ports. It sank right here."

"It seems that the potential perils presented by two gun decks and seventy-two heavy cannon were an oversight."

"I don't suppose there are life preservers aboard."

"No. Sink or swim."

Jean-Marc knew he had no choice. They boarded, and he admired the appointments in the main cabin. Fit for a king. And once they set sail, and had some privacy, the queen made him forget about the danger.

• • •

The day after the Queen of Sweden and Jean-Marc set sail, the pope arrived at Charles de Gaulle Airport on the north side of Paris. All arrangements had been made by his thorough and detail-oriented staff.

They were met by a sword and halberd-toting guard dressed in the period attire of long ago. A white pope-mobile constructed from an ancient carriage awaited he and his staff. The Swiss Guard deplaned with question marks indelibly inscribed on their expressions. Were they supposed to walk?

As the crowd pressed in to get a better look at the pope, his guardsmen formed a circle. What shouldn't have been expected was the crowd's reaction.

The Swiss Guard wore its traditional formal garb of bright colored, loose fitting uniforms with puffy shoulder adornments and flounced trousers. For all the crowd could determine, all twenty of them might just as well have piled out of a clown car at the circus.

Despite the crowd's expressed delight, the entourage set out for Notre Dame Cathedral many blocks away. No one dared to impede them. After all, the pope was a requisite to the impending coronation. And the French at this time, after being totally brainwashed by Mitim lore for the past two years, would let nothing stand in the way.

• • •

While the pope's ingress occurred, another landing took place southwest of Paris. The jet had just arrived to France from French Guiana. And Sylvain Lalumière was beside himself.

"Where are my clothes? My regalia? And why did our pilot announce arrival at Toussus-le-Noble airport? We went there in your covert mode, to attack Paris."

"There you have it. Covert mode. Yes, we landed there and snuck into Paris and attempted to place your little nuclear bomb in the Eiffel Tower. And we were confounded yet again by my former lover, Mag Crayle. Since I am quite good at sneaking, and sneaking is required, I am leading the way. No one shall see the new king and queen until we are both in our fineries and fully refreshed from our journey."

"Journey? Prison in Ushuaia, Argentina. Prison on Devil's Island, French Guiana. Hmph."

"Well, at least the Guiana was French. Right?"

"I am almost ready to take up religion so I can appeal to the benevolent God they talk about."

"We are landing at this airport because it supports general aviation. Commercial aircraft and their contents are not welcome. Less people to notice. We have a moment, here's a little history."

"I will try not to snore."

"Took our grouch pill this morning, did we? Well, here goes. I'll keep it brief. Toussus-le-Noble is the oldest airport in France. They used it during WW I and into WW II. But then the bad Germans took it over in 1940 and put those Stuka dive bombers here. For context, that Otto Von Prem Aryan type had one here. Refurbished to perfection. He had it taken to a military air museum near Xian, China. Are you getting the drift, here?"

"No."

"Von Prem was the one who picked it up there, added a mini-nuke in the carriage underneath, and then went to drop it on that Chin Yao-wu emperor, plus our French government in exile, who visited him at the Terra Cotta Warriors site."

"Incarceration does not do wonders for memories. Go on."

"Von Prem's back seat in the plane was the Iranian nuclear physicist who was kind of in charge of the bomb. He decided to commit *hara kiri* just to top off the day. All mentioned were toasted up in the many thousand degree heat when the bomb exploded. Almost got the Crayle team all in one fell swoop."

"Are we finished?"

"Wait. There's more. The USAAF Ninth Air Force grabbed the field ahead right after liberation."

"I will remember all that you've said in case the pope asks me history questions at my coronation."

"Eh, that would be *our* coronation."

Mercifully, the plane landed and the two prepared to depart.

"I cannot wear these prison rags. Someone will recognize me."

"You looked right at home on Devil's Island in that stained, charcoal-colored outfit. And I as one of the tarts that frequented the place. I've got it all figured out." She motioned to the now open door. "After you. And try not to look so tall."

Sylvain Lalumière stepped from the plane, stooped as if auditioning for a hunchback of Notre Dame role. He came to an abrupt stop.

"You are joking!"

He glared at a garbage truck that had pulled up nearby.

"It's perfect. I had it repainted. Royal purple with gold trim. And I had the interior of the back part redecorated. You'll love it."

With no more remarks left in his verbal quiver, Lalumière followed Pattie to the truck and climbed in through the back opening just before it ground shut.

He had to give her credit. The innards of the garbage truck were fit for a king. He laid on the floor and quickly fell asleep.

CHAPTER 42

The flight from Nova Scotia to Paris seemed longer than the actual five hours. No one was in a hurry and everyone aboard, save the pilots, needed and deserved a decent rest. With two of the CIA's best and most attentive pilots at the helm, they were assured the least turbulence possible. Magus Crayle stepped into the flight deck for a sitrep.

"Flori, we're nearing the coast of France. What's the weather look like west of Paris?"

"Ah, yes. Last time, when you climbed the Eiffel Tower to stop the Frenchman from planting and detonating one of those small nuclear devices, the electrical storm blew in from the west and caught you high up on the tower."

"Right before the New Years Eve fireworks went off. Yes, that was some night."

"But you succeeded. Paris was saved."

"We'll collect our Croix de Guerre another time. The weather?"

"I've tapped the display. *Non. Parfait.*"

"What? Does everybody else speak French?"

"You said, '*Croix de Guerre.*'"

"All right! All right! I give up."

"Ooh. Submission. I like that in a man."

"May I remind you that we are both quite happily married. There will be no restraining or—"

"*Ooh la la.* He knows about restraints."

"Ah!" Crayle turned and nearly ran into Hekka, who'd overheard the entire repartee.

"Nice game of chess, Flori. Now, about those restraints."

"Another time, perhaps."

• • •

Pre-touch-down, Flori re-verified the team's travel documents and distributed them back. Not long thereafter, she set the Bombardier Challenger 650 down at Paris Orly Airport eight miles south of the city center. Buffeting cross winds made the Crayle team's arrival somewhat of a Disneyland E-ticket event. Crayle, Hekka, Micmac, Lenny, and Alona each breathed a sigh of relief when the chirp of brakes signaled a safe landing. The three babies, also aboard and asleep, didn't indicate that anything at all had happened.

With the jet parked, Flori had some parting words for Crayle.

"I'd love to tag along and assist with the op. I'm not sure you're aware just yet, but Jack said he could detail me this time to help, if need be. He said the team seemed to have magic with the number six."

Although absent the deceased FBI Agent's Annie Oakley tag and the one-shot-between-the-eyes skill set, the Brazilian always qualified with ten-ring placements using her 9mm Beretta 92F relic. Being a military sidearm, it was large in size. She'd used it to justify with her husband, Jack Sommers, a much larger handbag. Prada, of course.

"We're just here to see that this king and queen thing comes off. And close the chapter with regard to Pattie and her husband.

A successful coronation implies no more nukes at least with respect to those two. A smaller playing field is a big deal with these kinds of weapons."

"I appreciate that," Flori said. "It's just that I received an in flight call. Darryl needs his plane back. While you're at the ceremony, I'll be swapping out this Challenger 650 for our usual 7X. Marli will have Jack's 8X in the vicinity. Just in case we need a split return."

"Sounds good."

• • •

They'd taxied to a stop a full three minutes before a French customs officer boarded. "Greetings from the government," he said. "Passports?"

Members of the team proffered the documents on cue.

"Your business in Paris?"

"Tourists." They gave the standard answer for any spy without diplomatic cover.

The customs agent picked out Crayle as the group's leader. "We are having a coronation tomorrow."

More than a leader of convenience, Crayle responded with an acting class acceptable rendition of astonishment. "Really? A coronation?"

"*Sacré bleu*. I thought the whole world knew," said the annoyed agent.

"Imagine the luck." Crayle high-fived the team.

"Where do you stay?"

"Hôtel Saint Louis en l'Isle." He spelled the ending.

"Eh, oui. The spelling before the revolution."

They'd stayed at the place before. Center city and only a short bridge traverse to Île Notre Dame next door and its famous cathedral.

"You must travel straight to your hotel. The coronation is tomorrow at noon. People are seeking their vantage points as we speak." He stamped each passport with a very special event stamp. He moved to each team member and, cheek-to-cheek, kissed the air in the French tradition. At that point, he smiled, waved, and departed. Once out of earshot, he muttered, "How could anyone not know?" He shrugged, and was gone.

They deplaned. Flori and her copilot had luggage lined up on the tarmac. A man attired in chauffeur garb tossed it all into the back of a shiny black stretch Hummer. The team piled inside into ultra-non-standard, swivel enabled Corbeau racing seats. The three babies were set up in miniature replicas of the seats. With little helmets placed on their heads, they appeared to be three of the up and coming Formula One prospects. And, they would work cheap.

They'd just started out when an empty middle seat at the rear tilted forward.

Heads swiveled. Hands went to smalls of backs and purses for weapons.

"*Bienvenue!*" announced the head that popped out. "Welcome!"

The team recognized the French-accented voice immediately. "Charleroi!" they chorused.

Crayle followed with a big smile and "*Bonjour, Monsieur! Comment ça va?*"

"It goes well, Mr. Crayle. The DGSE welcomes you all."

The French spy who'd played a major role in their last incursion into the City of Light pushed the seat back in place, and plopped down for the ride in. He provided commentary as he felt necessary of the sights along the way and remarked especially on the huge crowds expected for the next day's event.

"The French people are finally getting what they've wanted for the past two years. They come from all regions of the country. And from the rest of Europe. And, for that matter, from the rest of the world. There is hardly room for the media. And the police. Be very careful, my friends."

• • •

The team took in the sights on the way in. Porte D'Orléans—the city's southern entry point, Sorbonne—the famous university, Les Deux Magots—the restaurant of Ernest Hemingway fame, Musée D'Orsay—one of the world's most famous museums, and the bridge onto Île Notre Dame.

On this, the primary island in the middle of river Seine, sat the old Conciergerie, where Sylvain Lalumière's ancestors were incarcerated before being beheaded. Beyond, they caught a glimpse of the recreated and re-established Cathedral Notre Dame. Magnificent. Each paused for a moment. It was necessary. It was there that the tall Frenchman would achieve his indelible goal. To be crowned King of France.

Finally, the stretch Hummer traversed a bridge to the Île Saint Louis and to the front of their hotel, the amazing Hôtel Saint Louis en l'Isle. Bags inside, they bade a temporary farewell to their old friend and fellow spy, Charleroi.

A stickler for detail, Darryl had arranged for the team to have the same rooms as a year before. Familiarity was the spy's friend. Home.

It was time for a rest. Tomorrow would be a big day.

CHAPTER 44

The absence of the every-now-and-then Parisian ladies in their form-fitting LBDs went unnoticed on the auspicious day. Little black dresses were replaced by especially crafted period attire that would befit a Seventeenth Century Louis XIV-style coronation.

The wide sidewalks that outlined the Champs Élysées no longer sported the normally plentiful outdoor café seating designed for people watching. They filled with would be courtiers and even a few jesters, determined to make the wait bearable.

At 11 a.m., a furor overtook the crowd. All eyes spun in the direction of the grand Arc de Triomphe. There, those at the outer edge, or tall enough, spotted a horse-drawn carriage. An open air carriage. To their surprise, the driver, footman, and two occupants appeared in peasants clothing. Not the finery expected.

"*Oh la la!*" some exclaimed.

An Englishman translated. "Something is wrong!"

Sometimes what appears to be wrong is very, very right.

The man in the carriage stood as he passed the masses.

They gasped.

There he was. All six-foot-six inches of him.

And the mask.

The word, "*Mitim!*" exclaimed throughout, sounding like machine gun fire.

The French people had waited two solid years for this moment, never expecting even a glimpse. The dream became real.

Periodically, Lalumière pulled down the famous iron mask to reveal the man beneath. The folk hero of France. The king to be.

The carriage finished the Champs Élysées and turned onto the Pont au Change. The original, and more direct, route would have taken them over the Pont Notre-Dame. That bridge, one of the event planners discovered, had been called in street parlance Pont du Diable. The Devil's Bridge. Not good. And new choice indicated change. As from democracy to monarchy.

The Bateaux Mouches, boats used to transport sightseers on the Seine River, were poised below, filled to capacity. Then, the entourage and carriage arrived onto Île Notre Dame, and its eponymous, world-famous cathedral.

CHAPTER 45

The pews of Notre Dame Cathedral were packed. With the restoration, they were made comfortable and allowed parishioners a little extra room. The back of each one sported a video screen with Blue Tooth access for those with enabled ear pieces. Singing from hymnals, captured by hidden state-of-the-art microphones and produced over numerous loudspeakers, was even pitch-corrected in real time for those in need.

Special invitations of fully vetted attendees and strict entrance screening a full block from the site implied a peaceful, safe, and sanctified coronation.

Unarmed, and in the third row adjacent to the middle isle, sat the now five-member Crayle team.

There, just mere feet away, stood arch nemesis, Pattie. At Lalumière's side, she turned her head to peer straight into Crayle's eyes. She deployed her trademark point dimples as if to say, "Yes, Magus. I now have everything I've ever wanted. For all these years. Everything."

As she turned back, the cathedral's archbishop nodded. She knelt. He and the pope placed the gold crown.

"Rise, Patrice, Queen of all France."

The crowd maintained silence. Applause would be undignified during a coronation.

Then came Lalumière's turn.

"Before we continue, I have something to show the people of France."

The cleric was not prepared for the unscripted commentary.

His trepidation was for naught.

Lalumière pulled from his cloak a tissue-wrapped object. It was the object he'd discovered in his cell on Sainte Marguerite Island. The one left for him by Pattie after she'd left for Monte Carlo. When he believed that she'd perished there in the nuclear explosion.

He held it aloft so everyone could see, then peeled down the tissue.

There in his hand, sparkling in the stained-glass-filtered light, sat the famous Black Diamond. Guaranteed path to the throne.

The collective gasps reverberated throughout the cathedral.

Had there been any doubt as to the legitimacy of Sylvain Lalumière, it was henceforth put to rest.

Crayle could feel the emotions of the man. He'd decried the fatal outcomes of his forebears. Beheaded, every one. Pattie had seen and seized the opportunity. She'd recreated the personage of the Man In The Iron Mask legend. A man deserving to be King of France, yet deprived. A necessary harmony and equilibrium denied the people of his country.

"Kneel," the archbishop commanded.

Lalumière did so.

The pope placed the second, and most significant, gold crown.

"Rise," the clerics said in chorus. "Rise Louis Nineteen, King of France."

He did. And pivoted to the throng. This time it couldn't contain itself. It burst into applause and cheers. "*Vive Le Roi, Louis!*" they cried out. "*Vive La France!*"

The pope and the archbishop became obscured by the moment.

The new king took Pattie's hand and proceeded down the center aisle.

No one tried to touch the new king and queen. It was just as well. Three snipers hidden behind organ pipes high behind the altar were ready to take out anyone who did.

Great precaution, bad choice of venue. The pipes burst forth with Amazing Grace as the would-be protectors dropped their weapons and grabbed their heads.

On the way past row three, Pattie glanced a side look at Crayle. She mouthed three words.

Adept at lip reading from a former incarnation, Crayle swallowed hard. "I'm not done," she'd said.

He so needed it all to be over.

The crowd followed the pair out the large, double door entrance, to watch them board their royal carriage. Except it was only Lalumière.

Crayle glanced about. No Pattie. Strange.

Finished for the day, he led the other four alongside the Notre Dame cathedral. They passed its rear gardens where, a while back, he and Hekka had enjoyed a fine bottle of wine, and an excellent French cheese. He marched them toward the bridge to Île St. Louis.

• • •

It was over. Sylvain Lalumière, now King Louis XIX, had been transported away in a Louis XIV solid gold, open carriage. A victory lap of the Arc de Triomphe, followed by a short transfer to the recently rebuilt monarch residence at Versailles.

As the procession traversed the Champs Élysées in the opposite direction of that morning, the afternoon sun glinted off the king's new crown. One spectator cried out the obvious question, “Where is the queen?”

Lalumière smiled. “She’s gone ahead. She’s preparing my dinner.”

The crowd burst into communal laughter. They not only had a king, they had one with a sense of humor.

• • •

Back at Notre Dame, Team Crayle headed east toward the bridge that led to their hotel.

Crayle stopped halfway across. “Hold up, everyone.” He scanned behind. “Where’s Lenny?”

The team, being quite used to the French and their idiosyncrasies, shrugged. They performed their own furtive scans of the crowds. No Lenny.

“I’m going back,” Crayle decided. “See you back at the hotel.”

“Thank you, Mag,” Alona said. “When you find my twerp, tell him to expect Holy Hell when I see him. And tell him I love him.”

“See you in a few.” Their leader turned and headed upstream through the departing throngs.

CHAPTER 46

The coronation of Sylvain Lalumière and Pattie Norbrunn was in the books. The French news service, Le Monde, characterized the conversion of the government from a democracy back to a monarchy as a *fait accompli*. What they hadn't observed was that Magus Crayle seemed to have disappeared. Utilizing all of her CIA location apps and even a normal phone call, Hekka couldn't locate him anywhere. He'd gone to look for Lenny, but more than an hour had passed.

Reluctant, she turned to the CIA for assistance. She knew that Doctor Rorschach, the Agency's premier research psychiatrist, was still ardently working on communications between her husband's cochlear implant and the doctor's own computer. He answered on the second ring.

"*Ja*," he responded, recognizing her voice at once. "I haff the Chee-Pee-Ess vorking! Chust now!" An excited Rorschach always reverted to his Swiss-accented version of English.

"GPS?"

"*Ja, ja.*" He calmed for a moment. Back to unaccented English. "The old subcutaneous Vestige chip merely electronically engraved geographic coordinates onto nearby metal structures. My cochlear invention sends encrypted audio via satellite in both directions. Plus location. And finally, two years after embedding it in your husbands ear canal, it works!"

It appeared that Hekka had called at just the right time. She heard Jack Sommers in the background.

"There he is!" Jack cried out. "High five, Doctor. This will be a great addition to the CIA bag of tricks!"

"If those gear-heads in Science and Technology don't screw it up," Rorschach added.

A familiar voice broke through their celebration. "This is Hekka. Hello? Tell me where he is."

"Sorry. We vectored off," Jack said. He told her the coordinates that appeared on the doctor's travel computer. Jack touched. He appeared surprised, but related the location anyway. "Tell Magus 'Hi' for us."

"Will do. Oops, low battery. Going dark now." She hung up and switched off her Smartphone.

Before the two men could revert back to mutual congratulations, a different voice broke through, and presented itself on the computer speakers.

"You're mine now, Magus. You were captivated by me before... before her. Now, my captive. All mine."

Of the two men listening, Jack was the only one who recognized the voice. Even though he clapped his free hand over his mouth, a muffled exclamation escaped.

"*Pattie!*"

Minutes of silence later, Jack regained his senses. "Hekka is no match for Pattie! Get Micmac! Get that French spy, Charleroi!"

"I am a psychiatrist, Mr. Sommers. I cannot get anyone."

"Right. Right." Jack grabbed his Smartphone. He placed two desperate calls.

CHAPTER 47

Earlier, in search of Lenny, Crayle walked through the doorway of the Notre Dame cathedral. No guard. No cleric. Just an open door way. He proceeded through the spacious nave giving a glance ahead and to either side. No one. Empty.

His quarry, Lenny Lipschitz, could be difficult to locate sometimes. Other times, just difficult. Crayle found a door, knocked and pushed it open.

The room he entered was twenty feet wide by thirty feet deep. All walls were a creamy white except the far one.

A mural covered it in its entirety. He recognized the scene. It was the bar and restaurant in Cannes. On the French Riviera. The outside patio, round tables, and chairs facing the bus station and the boat harbor had his mind connecting the dots.

Something moved. It was not a mural. It was a giant flat screen. A young woman stepped in from the right. He recognized her immediately. Pattie Norbrunn.

"I'm not sure about congratulations, Pattie, but I'm hoping your ascendance to Queen of France means no more killings." His restored memories had long ago connected those dots. He'd first met her in Paris as Crayle One, the CIA assassin.

She took a seat. "Hello, Magus. It's been some time. Hasn't it?"

He started to take a seat opposite.

But something was wrong. In the short time since the coronation, she'd doffed her Queen of France attire and donned something more usual to her.

He exited his dumbfounded state when he noticed motion in his peripheral vision. It seemed that the far wall inched toward him. He shook his head and turned his focus back to her.

"You will remember this." She stood and unzipped the mini-dress, allowing it to drop to the floor. There, standing completely nude, she produced her trademark smile. The little point dimples perhaps an inch from each end of her mouth served as punctuation for his increased heart rate.

The wall, now ten feet away, brought him back to physical reality. He spun on his heel to face a completely blank wall. No door. He spun back.

"Finally, you are mine," she said as she resumed her seat.

The image grew ever larger as the wall pressed toward him.

Lights flicked on in the video as the sun bid adieu. The typical evening fog for the northern Mediterranean port city approached from the left.

He was trapped.

"Don't worry, my love. We aren't finished. Not yet."

Three feet.

Two.

He pushed behind, trying to turn. Then, he noticed.

It wasn't a fog on the video screen coming from the old Cannes port. It was a mist filling the shallow remaining space.

As it penetrated his nose and mouth, his head became heavy. More and more until it banged forward against the encroaching video screen just about to crush him.

The camera zoomed in. Just her blood red lips now. Forming a kiss.

They formed words. No sound.

Just her lips.

"Sweet dreams."

His mind, not the video, faded to black.

He slid sideways as the friction of the screen in front, and the wall behind, slowed his fall. He lay motionless.

• • •

Crayle awoke in a different room. No video mural. No moving wall. No drug-infused fog. No Pattie Lalumière.

He found himself bound to a solid gold Louis XIV throne, wrists and ankles, and his chest strapped to the chair back. Both immobile and stark naked, he surveyed the room for answers.

Pattie was there. He smelled her presence.

She stepped around from behind. And knelt to his left. She ran the backs of her fingernails from his knee slowly along the tender flesh inside his thigh. Then, in reverse only with the nails scraping, engaging the many nerve endings.

"It won't work," he said.

"Of course it will. I will appeal to all of your masculine senses. Your body will respond. And I will sit on your lap and take advantage."

"You are crazy. I have someone … someone who doesn't deserve this. Go to your husband … or his son. You don't need sex from me."

"Oh, it's not about the sex. You see, I'm off the pill. And today is the peak of my cycle, Magus."

"No, no! Oh, no! You … you can't!"

"Oh, but I can. I will take you and I will capture your seed."

"*No!*"

"You are a mastermind. You get how diabolical I am. I shall become pregnant. By you."

"You were insane before Hekka came along. This isn't about jealousy."

"Heavens, no. Your beautiful wife has been the perfect competition. In fact, I expect to meet with her. To be with her. Quite soon. Of course, I won't tell her that it was you who impregnated me. She'll be all happy thinking it's Sylvain … or maybe Jean-Marc. Don't you just love the irony?"

He didn't have words.

"Don't worry. Not yet. I have something to do before we, you know, do our thing. I'll be back in just a little. You can practice in your mind not to respond to my touch. And my sexual allure. I do love a challenge. But you know that, don't you?"

With that, she donned her little black mini-dress, and exited via the royal doorway. At Versailles.

• • •

Pattie returned an hour later, walked over to her captured Magus Crayle, and got down on her knees. "You're already aware that my mother was a prostitute. I would peek through a keyhole when she did things to her customers. I learned a lot. How to make men respond."

She drew her finger nails once more along his inner thigh.

"You killed her."

"She decided to give up my purity to gratify the twisted desires of that CIA mole. She made me call him Mr. Wohlford."

"You killed him, too."

"I got justice with both of them."

"It brought out your dark side. You learned to kill just for the pleasure of it. Justice no longer figured into the equation."

"I think you're right. You always did see things more clearly. Killing my husband, Randy, and that Swiss banker felt like I'd taken drugs. Super powerful wonderful drugs."

"And Wohlford's wife. The French-Canadian."

"I lost track after a while."

Crayle knew he had to keep the conversation going, but he'd not had a class in talking to a psychopath during his CIA schooling at The Farm in the Virginia countryside. "Tell me about your future. As you see it. I want to hear. When you're finished, tell me about mine."

She smiled her dimpled smile. "Your future begins… right now."

Pattie walked to a hearth. Like everything else in the palace, a reconstruction of all that she'd obliterated with a bomb. She picked up a log lighter, and paced to a set of quite beautiful, Louis XIV drapes.

"I believe I saw you shiver a moment ago."

Kneeling to the floor, she made a point of deliberately setting the material on fire. She stood and walked to the others in the room, and set them ablaze as well.

It seems the proud French men and women involved in the reconstruction of the Versailles Palace had been too proud to use the less splendiferous but fireproof drapes specified. They'd stood back, and admired the product of their little secret.

Somehow, Pattie knew that.

CHAPTER 48

"Welcome to Hell, Magus. I've taken your comfort into consideration. I've turned the air conditioning up to max."

He felt the alternating searing and freezing air currents.

"I suppose recommending you seek professional help is somewhere beyond pointless."

"What could anyone help me with? Sex? You know how good I am. Strategy and tactics? Same. Dirty tricks? Ditto." She shrugged.

"I'll concede those. It's the psychotic behaviors." He coughed up the smoke. "Let's go somewhere where we can talk."

"So you can seduce me … again?"

"No one's ever seduced you. You'd kill them if they did."

"But only after the sex. Right?"

"That seems to be your M.O." He anticipated what he was certain would come next.

"It was me in Louisville. But you know that."

Needing to remain calm, he choked back the emotions. And thoughts of Phoebe's final moments.

"They didn't find a body. But you knew that."

"The FBI ran forensics on the hotel room—the crime scene. The technician remarked that she'd found the clearest, most well-defined left index finger print in her twenty-seven years. Positive ID."

"A message."

"The message was for me. You used your left finger because I'm left-handed. You knew I'd notice. Then you sent Phoebe's Glock to signify her death. The print was the salutation."

"How I do love an intact mind."

"Pattie, shoot me. Stab me with your unholy cross. Leave Hekka be. Take your own life so you can join me. In Hell!"

"What a fabulous idea. Only one problem. I'm in love with her. Don't you see? I'll protect her forever."

"Leave her alone, for Chrissakes!"

"No can do. My mother, in her profession, had to please whoever walked through the door."

"And you watched."

"I educated myself. I'm ready to go there … and take your beautiful Hekka with me."

It had taken precious time. At least, he knew Hekka was still alive.

The heat reached unbearable.

Sweat poured off the both of them.

Crayle had to really become the Magic Man. He had to kill Pattie now.

He pulled with all his strength until the Velcro ties cut deep into his wrists.

"Don't you get it, Magus? The flames represent Hell. The A/C stands for A Cold Day."

"A Cold Day In Hell. That should make the *it'll be's* happy."

Pattie pinched her eyebrows together. "It'll be's?"

"They go around saying, It'll be a cold day in Hell as if they know that something that can happen, won't."

"Love your mind, Magus. Is it warm enough for you?"

So intense was the situation, neither heard pounding on the door. Or noticed it spring open because the heat had warped the door frame.

It was intuition.

On Pattie's part. She snatched her pistol off a nearby table.

She turned just in time to witness Hekka in full motion.

Coming toward her, stopping just ten feet away.

There Crayle was. Wrists and ankles fastened. In front, he beheld Hekka holding her ten-inch Bowie. Faced off against Pattie with a handgun.

"Knife to a gunfight, my darling. I'm truly sorry."

Pattie took a few steps toward her.

Crayle worked his feet together, loosening one shoe and then catapulting it ahead of Pattie's path toward Hekka..

The shoe bounced once before Pattie's foot landed on it.

Stepping on the shoe threw her off. She swung her arms wide to catch her balance, taking the gun off point blank at Hekka.

Hekka lunged.

The ten-inch Bowie knife seemed to pierce the flames as if thrust by the Devil instead of a Serrano goddess.

Thunk!

It impaled Pattie to the hilt.

Eyes wide, mouth open, Pattie gasped, "I, I have you. But. You, you've broken my heart, darling."

With purpose, Hekka uttered two of Magus' favorite words, "Figuratively … and literally."

She dropped her guard too soon.

Pattie latched onto Hekka's shoulders, and tried to pull them together. The Bowie's substantial hilt denied that eventuality.

At first, her lips quivered. Then, with force of purpose, morphed into a full smile. Dimples and all.

She leaned up on her tip toes as if to supply a kiss.

"I … I … love …"

Pattie Norbrunn Lalumière, ultra rogue CIA agent and newly crowned queen of all France, brushed the Serrano as she collapsed forward.

A subtle twist in the air, and the Crayles heard the thunk as the body slammed and the protruding three inches of blade impaled itself into the ancient wood floor board.

Anxious moments passed.

They half expected Pattie to leap to her feet, pull the knife free, and go on the attack.

It didn't happen.

Hekka knelt. She closed the eerily staring eyes.

Then stood, looking down at their dead nemesis.

She placed her foot on Pattie's chest, and extracted the Bowie. She cleaned off the blood on the hem of the dead rogue agent's LBD, used it to free her husband, then dropped it into her elongated Prada handbag.

He ran over to his clothes, neatly folded and stacked by Pattie, and dressed. "You know, we'd be in trouble if she hadn't left my shoes on."

"Bet she'd like to have that one back."

Crayle offered final words. "I'm not much for quoting scripture, or even remembering it. Even if it didn't, it should've read, *And God said, watch out for this one!*"

The fire alarm blared at a deafening pitch. It wrested them from their mesmerizing moment just past and into their urgent present.

He grabbed her hand. She pulled free.

"Mag . . . we've just killed the Queen of France! Right here in Paris. In Versailles!"

He got the magnitude of what just happened. "We're out of here!"

He pulled the relevant fire alarm handle on the nearest wall, anyway.

The two were through the door.

With not a moment to lose, they escaped the conflagration.

"Where'd you get that?" Crayle said, indicating the Prada.

"I put it on the card. Only an extra $4,000 for the extended length."

"You don't have a card with that kind of oomph."

"Thanks be to Jack Sommers."

"You still have his Black Card?"

Apropos of Paris, she just shrugged.

• • •

Outside and across the street, the two heard the klaxons of sirens just a couple of blocks away.

They turned to see the palace that was Versailles.

"The fire is temporary. The *pompiers*—firefighters—will have it out in no time," Crayle surmised.

"True. But Pattie's fire, her Hell, is eternal."

• • •

Crayle motioned to Hekka, then ducked into an empty alley. He used a virtual sat phone app on his Smartphone to order an exfil post haste. Jack directed them to a secluded airport southwest of Paris. He added that they could expect to find the team's usual ride, the Dassault Falcon 7X replete with Flori, refueled and ready.

On the way, Crayle rang up Micmac. The time for closure was always ASAP. According to Micmac himself.

The former SEAL answered. They validated via a verbal handshake derived from a very old Skeeter Davis song.

"Don't they know ..."

"... it's the end of the world."

Crayle filled him in on the coronation aftermath.

"Micmac. Pattie's dead. She confessed to Louisville. And Phoebe."

He listened to a moment of silence.

"I'm pretty choked up right now, Mag. Thanks for the sitrep."

He finished with, "It may be of little consequence to you right now, but Phoebe can truly rest in peace."

• • •

Later, Hekka and Crayle found their own moment of peace and quiet. He spoke first.

"How'd you find me?"

"I asked the obvious question. Where in Paris would Pattie be? That's when I saw smoke rising from Versailles Palace. I put Sister Magdalena, Pattie's alter ego, together with that."

After an irrepressible chuckle, Crayle mused, "Now, what was that about bringing a knife to a gunfight?"

CHAPTER 49

Walking along the Paris street, Hekka and Crayle noticed a crowd of people huddled in front of a store. It appeared that the store sold televisions and had placed six in the front window, facing outward.

They pressed in close enough to see the picture on the center unit. Lalumière. The newly crowned King of France lay as if in state. He wore his full regalia from the coronation.

The surrounding five sets turned on. Each with the same video feed.

It was Pattie and Lalumière in a bedroom *in flagrante*, as the Italians would say.

The crowd, though very French, gasped. They stood transfixed as the motion increased along with the intensity of the act. It was very clear when the session was complete. Both participants had clearly arrived at their destinations.

Crayle whispered in Hekka's ear. "Let's get out of here. We might pop up next."

Then, something neither of them expected.

Screams from the crowd.

People emitting anguished cries.

"*Mon Dieu!*"

"*Il est finis!*"

And, finally, someone summed it up.

"*Le Roi est mort!*"

"My God, Hekka! The king is dead! Pattie killed him!"

The people continued to watch.

Hurrying away, the Crayles heard what sounded like a group exhale, and turned.

All of the people stared directly at them.

They ran.

Crayle and Hekka were in excellent shape. They could run a mile at a fair clip.

The French, used to gourmet meals and fine wines, could not.

"While I was captured," Crayle said as he huffed and puffed. "Pattie left for an hour. That's when she did it!"

"Both of them, then. Gone."

"And somehow, she put up her murder video, followed by images of us."

"They think we did it . . . murdered their king."

"And queen."

The pair eluded the chasers and reached Pont au Change, leading to Île Notre Dame. Hurrying past the Conciergerie, both took a breath with the knowledge that those awaiting the guillotine during the post-revolution Reign of Terror included some of Sylvain Lalumière's relatives. It was that incentive that kicked off the entire French component of the war the Crayle team had fought for the past couple of years.

They heard sounds a couple of blocks behind. Angry mob sounds.

Passing by the Notre Dame cathedral and across the single connecting bridge, they reached the other of the two mid-Seine islands, Île Saint Louis.

A short walk and they spun right, into their residence for the coronation, the Hôtel Saint Louis en l'Isle. As already noted, they'd been at this place a year before. When Lalumière and his gang had tried to nuke the entire French government leadership by planting and igniting one of the Made In China devices up on the Eiffel Tower. The Crayle team had spoiled the whole show.

"I believe we've checked out. We'd like the room from before," Crayle said as he arrived at the front desk.

"*Oh la la*," said the clerk.

Crayle extended a hand, proffering a one thousand euro note.

"Right away, Monsieur."

Shortly after her husband filled in the blank, Hekka turned the key and they entered the room.

"Just as we left it," Crayle observed.

"Except for one thing."

"What?"

"The bed covers aren't all over the room."

She locked the door and turned to see her husband already half undressed. "So, you think my name, Hekka, is Finnish for *sure thing*?"

"If that mob catches up with us, this could be our last time!"

Her heartbeat ramped. His, too.

She started to disrobe, but paused a moment, conjuring an inquisitive look. "So, I was your first. Right?"

Post Rorschach's full restore, Crayle had no difficulty remembering previous women. But his rational mind intercepted a full and truthful response before it could reach his lips. He had an epiphany. "Well, there was this girl in Philadelphia."

"That's a Bond line."

He produced a French shrug.

"Come here."

He stepped close.

"About those specific memories? I'm going to see that you lose them. All of them."

CHAPTER 50

Earlier, Lenny had waited until Notre Dame emptied. He approached the dais. "Excuse me. Pope, Sir? You married my wife and I at the CIA's underground cathedral in Washington, D.C.? Remember?"

The pope, at first concerned about his safety, recovered at the sight of the diminutive personage before him. The one in Belle Epoque period attire and wearing a backpack. "Of course. Mr. Lipschitz. Lenny, if I may?"

"You certainly may. I just wanted to congratulate you on a wonderful ceremony... and ask a little question, if *I* may. It's a religious question, so I think you can handle it."

The pope remembered the man, indeed. This was the one who, with extreme spontaneity, could turn a pleasant conversation otherwise. "Yes. I do have a little experience in that area. Your question?"

"You realize that I'm asking you to pontificate. Right?" Lenny waited in vain. "Pontiff? Pontificate?"

The pope pondered. Humor was one of the many blessings the Creator had bestowed on the human race. How could it go so wrong?

It didn't take Lenny long to interpret the papal glare he received. "Okay, then. Well, I'm Jewish. Christians say you have to accept Jesus as your savior before you can get into heaven."

"Yes?"

"Is there a way around that?"

"I believe that to be the least of your worries."

Before the pope could finish the thought, a cardinal rushed in. "We have bad news, Your Eminence. The Holy aircraft is disabled. It can't be repaired for two days. I'm sorry."

"Oh, no. I have an event in Jerusalem tomorrow. A meet with Israel's top cleric. Can you put me on private charter? Or on a commercial flight?"

"Uh, not possible. With the huge crowds attending the coronation now heading out…"

Lenny jumped in. "I've got a plane. Ready right now. You spring for the gas on the way, I'll get you there."

"A miracle! I shall devise a special blessing. In your honor."

"Forget that. Just get me into heaven. When my time comes."

The pope quickly brushed aside his next thought.

CHAPTER 51

It was a new day in Paris. The team, minus Alona, assembled in the Crayles' room to discuss what had gone before, and what they should do next. Right away, they unanimously agreed to pack their bags, fetch a ride back to the airport Jack had specified, and fly home. It seemed simple. Until Alona called on the room phone.

"I still haven't seen Lenny. Not a word from him, either. I've checked the storage in the room. His backpack is gone. I'm really worried that something…" She became emotional and hung up.

Before they could react, Micmac's tablet computer flashed a video onto the previously black screen. Its sleep mode could only be awakened by what computer technology experts labeled as priority interrupts. This was one such instance.

He quickly recognized the scene. He was virtually viewing out the windshield of a Dassault Falcon 7X jet. "What my visualization goggles don't do," he complained. "is indicate who is wearing them. It could be either of the pilots. Aside from that little oversight, the high definition resolution is better than the human eye."

Just then, the door opened and in walked Marli, one of Jack Sommers' two pilots. The computer display caught her eye. Micmac noticed.

"My powers of deduction lead me to believe that Flori is at the helm. Trying out my new gadget. Jack give you the day off?"

"That my ex-husband, Jack, might prefer her in certain circumstances is well known. But..."

Following behind and shutting the door, the referenced Brazilian beauty checked the disbelieving stare on Micmac's countenance.

"What?"

His head spun back to the screen. "Then, who is flying the 7X?"

The women closed in, taking positions, to peer over his shoulders.

Flori's face blanched. "That Saint Christopher on the dash. It's mine! That's my 7X!"

The view through the goggles lowered from the window to the pilot's lap.

"That's my remote controller!" Micmac exclaimed.

"Who would fly our jet by remote except you?" Flori asked.

Micmac recalled that, for lack of space in his own room, he'd asked Lenny to store it for him. Maybe in the backpack he seemed to tote everywhere.

Crayle dove in. "All we know now is, your device and our 7X are gone!"

In an uncharacteristic panic, he called Alona.

She picked up on the first ring. "That you, Lenny? If—"

"No. It's me," Crayle interrupted. "Alona, check again for Lenny's backpack."

"What's he done? Never mind." She rechecked the closet. "Not there. Maybe he's off on a long hike. Baby and I are coming over."

"The door's unlocked," Crayle advised. He clicked off.

Alona and her baby arrived three minutes later to find the rest enraptured by the computer display.

Crayle turned to the women. "It's him! By God, it's him!"

"Look! There on his thigh! He just touched it! It's Phoebe's hair braid!"

"Lenny!" Alona cried out. "She was big sister to him!"

"OMFG! He grabbed the jet and is using your auto-fly prototype gadget!"

"Right, Marli. Can you pick up the location? Latitude? Longitude?"

Micmac entered a 'back door' code. "Let's take a deep breath."

In unison, they did.

"There. Lat. Long. Altitude. Direction. Speed."

He clicked an icon.

"He's crossing Jordanian airspace... into Saudi. Mag. Get the president on the line. He could have cleared an over-flight of those allies."

Crayle made quick work of it. He touched in the speed dial number on his phone. The others could only hear his side of the conversation.

"Yes, Kimbel. It's me. Sorry for the oh-dark-thirty call. We're still in Paris. We have a situation." He explained, waited, then listened. "Yes. I'll inform you if anything happens that you should know." He turned to the others.

"The president said it was requested as a mercy flight. The requestor used the term MGHM. As in, May God Have Mercy. Then, Kimbel went into a tizzy. Upset. Said the Iranians just broke the missile treaty again. They'd just launched another ICBM test."

Micmac sat back stunned. "Not good."

• • •

Heading east from an Israeli airbase, Lenny already knew the Iranians were about to fake an ICBM test. And launch for real. He'd placed a bug on the pope's garment, then listened in on the Israeli leader's conversation with him, the one interrupted by a Mossad intel officer.

Lenny was sure. The missile was loaded. A high-yield nuclear warhead. He was sure of one other thing. Target: Israel.

• • •

Flori looked up from her Smartphone. "I just did the math. He'll be running on fumes soon."

Crayle delivered the unwanted, but only, conclusion. "It's out of our hands."

Alona couldn't take it. "No, Lenny…"

She gave a slow shake of her head—side-to-side. She grasped the magnitude of what he was about to do. Even if they had communications, there would be no talking him out of it.

• • •

Lenny still received feed from the satellite-enabled bug in the pope's garment. New intel. Mossad now indicated from a hack into the Iranian command and control system. He repeated the words.

"The target is not, say again, not Israeli."

In the next moment, he relaxed. As he began to reverse direction, the bug went live once more.

"It's headed for Mecca!"

"That makes no sense," the pope cried out.

"In the darkest of ways," said the Israeli leader, "it does. They'll blame it on us. A war to end all wars.

The pope gasped at the thought. He breathed out the word.

"Armageddon."

CHAPTER 52

By now the Crayle team had all manner of intel coming in. CIA, NSA, DIA, MI6, DGSE, and Mossad.

They watched the 7X initiate a turn, then resume course.

Alona found her steady, grounded voice. "Do it. Little Lenny will be proud of his dad. A Mensch. With a capital M."

The goggle view turned to the co-pilot seat.

There sat the backpack.

Besides the temporary storage of Micmac's new business jet controller, since the Auckland incident it had housed the mini-nuke Lenny stole from the Eden Stadium soccer pitch. He'd saved the game and perhaps several hundred thousand innocent victims. The view went back to the window, then his lap. There, next to the braid Phoebe had kept to remember her father, sat a newer version of the CIA's Universal Remote Control.

A missile trail came into view. High above Lenny's altitude. Ahead, he approached the Red Sea. He pressed a button.

The computer screen flashed to black.

• • •

With the flash of light and the subsequent screen blackout, Alona lost control.

Tears burst from her eyes and flowed down her cheeks.

Her hands pressed hard to her cheeks as she cried.

Through bleary eyes, she saw her tears spatter on Little Lenny. Like drops of rain. The baby's face contorted, as in a first-time experience of fear.

Quick, Alona grabbed a loose end of her baby's blanket. She dabbed at her tears. The baby was about to join her. About to cry.

"No, no, no, no!" Alona wailed.

She wiped both sides of her face. Then, the baby a final time.

She brought her head erect, and re-instilled the unwavering pride she had. For Lenny. Her husband. Her hero.

• • •

The display in the sky high above Mecca had people hiding their eyes from the extremely bright flash. In the next instant, a witnessing cleric proclaimed it the inspiration of Allah.

Because the bomb hidden in Lenny's backpack was directional, and aimed for its force to extend forward and upward, there was little impact on the ground.

Lenny's bomb vaporized the missile from Iran, which sported its only operational nuclear weapon. At the same time, it obliterated the Aryan's rogue missile as well. And the Illuminé's final warhead.

Most of those who learned about the event in the coming days became inspired and committed to peace. The Israelis. The Iranians. Others around the world. It was clear to all but a few that the one God required absolute peace between the three religions … or else!

CHAPTER 53

The explosion over the Middle East was over. The coronation of a new king and queen of France, over. The surprise advent of a new replacement king, Jean-Marc Lalumière, likewise complete. Still in Paris, Crayle and Micmac shared a moment at their hotel.

"Well, my sailor friend, the intelligence agencies of the United States, like those around the world, are operating at warp speed after the explosive event over the Middle East. They'd missed everything. The rogue nuclear warhead missile fired from Israel. The similar device launched over Saudi Arabia's northern aspect from Iran.

"Yeah, and President Stones couldn't pass on your relevant experiences in South America. Off-the-books means precisely that. The situation was potentially dire. So, what precisely does our little Team Crayle have up its sleeve."

"I'd love to declare a time out right now. But…"

"Well, Mag, sending the ladies and babies on a Parisian shopping trip with Jack's Black Card was a stroke of genius. But, I can read you by now. What's on your mind that requires the two of us sequestered in your hotel room?"

"Look at this, Micmac." Crayle pointed to a computer that sat on their room's coffee table. "The nuke air burst from Lenny's backpack caused armies, navies, and air forces to jump to high alert. Right about DEFCON 4.5."

"I'm not surprised. They didn't see this one coming. Every country worries that they could be next. The media could even blame those countries by mistake."

"And as soon as one media outlet shoots that out, the rest are right on its heels."

"No one wants to get behind on so-called breaking news. They don't fact check or corroborate anymore."

"Like the five air blasts leading toward Big Bear."

"Right. News hysteria. What can we do?"

"Solutions require a problem definition, solution attributes, criteria, constraints, et cetera."

"Right in your systems methodology wheelhouse."

"My wheelhouse requires time. We're at the precipice. The slightest error in judgment somewhere can set it off."

"It?"

"That biblical outcome. Armageddon."

"How much time do you need?"

"More than we have."

"Shortcuts?"

"Those bring risks. Sometimes incalculable."

"You have the knowledge and experience in this problem solving shit. You say. We do."

"Okay. Systems Approach. Without the esoterica. Let's back this off a bit. Say the world's militaries are at DEFCON Five minus one. We need to give them a reason to stand down."

"BS won't do, will it?"

"No. What we give them has to be true and—that's a big and—they all must believe it straight away."

"Sure. For two guys with our creds and no time on the clock, piece of cake. Why don't you and I just win the Stanley Cup, the Super Bowl, and the World Series, and take the afternoon off?"

"That might be easier. Okay, something's just jumped into my mind. It can't possibly work."

Micmac entered ID and password on his computer, and channeled boss Jack Sommers. "Rock and Roll!"

"There are two social media giants. The California one we'll designate as A. The other one, B. They're the influencers. Create accounts for each."

"Names?"

"Lenny... and Phoebe."

Micmac looked up. "In their honor. By God, they even fight from the grave."

"We post radical stuff on each. Far right."

"A and B will shut down their accounts in a heartbeat."

"Exactly."

Micmac did as Crayle proscribed. Thirty minutes later, the accounts had gone live, and been suspended.

"Now, my Navy friend. Send the following to these addresses." He showed what he'd scribbled during the thirty minute account setup period.

"Where'd you get these instant message addresses?"

"While you worked, I stepped into the bathroom. Made a call. They're direct panic lines for decision makers at A and B."

"And when I send these texts?"

"Each of them will believe the other can scoop them by re-enabling our accounts first."

"So, without thinking, they enable and... "

"Then our message, our true story, goes via those SM giants to the world." Crayle placed a message he'd written in the bathroom next to Micmac's computer. "Note that our brand new accounts have no friends and that all external postings are disabled. Only our single post will show on the timeline."

Micmac entered the text on the new accounts. "Done. Posted. And the instant messages?"

Crayle took a seat next to him. "Send!"

The former SEAL pressed ***Enter***, sending the instant messages to A and B.

Almost instantly, each of the social media giants re-enabled the Lenny and Phoebe accounts. The following text shot round the world.

"Those two intercontinental ballistic missiles were launched by rogue entities. One initially targeted Israel, but then was retargeted to Mecca. The Iranian leader, now deceased Grand Ayatollah Fahsolah, obtained the nuclear warhead from a secret society self-describing itself as Aryan. The perpetrators decided that using their one atomic device on Israel would invoke retaliation by that country. Hitting Mecca and blaming Israel would turn the Muslim world, and likely most of the rest of the world, against Israel. Including the United Nations. Another warhead, sent by rogues in Israel itself, has been traced to the same source. These were the only two. To reiterate, the warheads themselves were neither Israeli nor Iranian.

"A jet aircraft flown by American, Lenny Lipschitz, was utilized by him to explode both missiles and their nuclear content in the air, thus saving the iconic center of religion from certain obliteration.

"The preceding information has been fully vetted and independently corroborated as accurate and credible."

The two sat back.

Much to their surprise and satisfaction, the so-called mainstream media picked up the story 'as is' and ran with it. Full bore.

"Every once in a while you throw the Hail Mary."

"And it works."

• • •

In the following hours, the world stood down.

"We're not finished," Crayle advised his friend.

"What? Everyone's spinning down. DEFCON Four to DEFCON One in a little over an hour. Isn't that enough?"

"Not quite. They've bought the package. We need to add the 'but wait' kicker."

They did. The two newly created accounts posted for the second and final time.

"Just in! Lenny Lipschitz, the man who recently saved the Middle East and quite possibly the world, was Jewish!"

Micmac saw Crayle's intention. Sometimes even the most unlikely individual can make a serious, positive difference. "Phoebe would have liked that."

"Secretly."

"Of course."

• • •

In the following weeks, the world media finally got it right. Lenny became the hero. Saudi Arabs and the Iranians, with their new leader, found cause for peace. Enduring peace. Lenny's legacy was given a king's welcome in the emirate known as Dubai.

"Lenny was Jewish!" one media outlet declared.

"Our Lenny saved Mecca!" came a competitor's response.

The battle was on.

"He did it! Lenny did it!"

"World peace is next!"

"Heaven help us!"

Lenny became trademarked, copyrighted, and claimed as a previously unknown contributor to every media outlet.

One television pundit went so far as to end his show as he'd never done before. With something appropriate.

"Lenny Lipschitz. Rest In Peace."

CHAPTER 54

The remainder of the team exfiltrated via the remaining Falcon 8X back to America. Back in their Big Bear Valley. In spite of the five nuclear airbursts to the west, they found everything intact save for the loss of Phoebe and Lenny. They'd have instantly given up their cabins and possessions to get their colleagues and exceptionally close friends back.

Crayle, Hekka, and their baby sat on their cabin's back deck on a finc early Winter morning. New Years Eve was a day away, but they didn't expect to feel like celebrating.

"Hey, Mag. I need to run down to the Quarry and pick up my mother. Wanna come?"

"Yeah. Sure. What could go wrong? It just seems that everywhere we go, shtuff happens."

"Shtuff?"

"Lenny created a new word, and shared it with me. Alona forbids swearing anywhere near their baby. It means—"

"I can guess what it means. C'mon. Spending time in a covert hospital 300 feet beneath a rock quarry with a mad psychiatrist can be wearying. Let's go rescue my mom."

"To make it quick, we'll take the Cobra."

"Yes. A two-seater. And how are you getting back?"

"We'll take your car."

The trip down from the Big Bear Valley plateau was quick, as promised, and exhilarating. Hekka slowed her fully-restored, bright yellow Ford Bronco to a crawl across the quarry gravel and into the special garage. A few minutes in the express elevator, and they arrived.

"Let's surprise the good doctor." They walked in. There Doctor Rorschach stood, Hekka's mother holding one hand. The other, held by a tallish woman with light Auburn hair.

Crayle glanced back and forth, then back over to Hekka. She sported the same minimalist smile he fell in love with so many months before. She knew.

Then, he glanced back at someone gone from his life and memories for so long.

"Hekka, allow me to introduce my mother."

• • •

The team shared lunch in the minimal and efficient hospital cafeteria. The four of them bade *au revoir* to Doc Rorschach and headed back up the hill. Home.

Hekka drove and chatted with her mother while Crayle and his own mother started a catch up process that would take months. They arrived, retired to respective sleeping quarters, and napped most of the afternoon.

• • •

After a couple of hours of restful and necessary sleep, Crayle awoke to find Hekka gone from the bedroom. He threw on his usual black cargo shorts and matching T-shirt, and headed to the living room.

There on the sofa sat both mothers, plus recent arrivals, Micmac and Alona, gazing out the big windows at the now treeless back yard, the boat dock, and Big Bear Lake. Serenity seemed to be the order of the day.

As he approached, he first heard, then saw, Hekka. She sat cross-legged on the floor, her back to him, reading from something on her lap. With three enrapt babies, each in its own bouncer seat, facing her, he imagined the story to be a fairy tail. But what he heard caused him to think she was accessing her creative side.

"In the East, there came Three Wise Men. One Israeli, one Persian, and one Christian. They were known as the Magi. It means wise men. The Latin plural of Magus."

She looked up to be sure that at least one of the babies was still awake. To her surprise, they all appeared focused on her every word.

"The leader of Israel. The leader of Iran. The Pope. They chose the route they'd take from Rome. From Jerusalem. From Tehran. To finish in Bethlehem. For the second coming. And then, there would be peace."

Hekka placed what he expected to be a book of fiction on the coffee table next to her.

It was a newspaper. Today's newspaper.

Crayle caught his breath. It was real.

He stepped over to Jack's wall of collector plates. Probably forty of them, they'd been shattered by machine gun fire during a cabin assault, and miraculously resurrected. Then, smashed by the eighty-foot pine blown down in the back yard by attacking, explosive-packing drones. They'd staged a comeback from that one, as well. They appeared good as new. There'd been someone way back in history that had done that. Someone no one could destroy. The dish right in front of him caught his attention. It proffered the message.

PEACE.

• • •

Magus Crayle's mesmerized moment staring at the collector's plate was shattered by the ringing of the doorbell. That he moved from tomorrow's potential to today's reality in a few steps wasn't lost on him.

Not expecting anyone, he checked the video on his special Smartphone. It didn't do for a spy to peer out a standard door peephole, block the light from inside, and give the wrong people an easy shot through or below that so-called security device.

Instead, he stood with his back to a sidewall. He couldn't believe what he observed. He shook the phone. Checked again. Same visual.

By now, he suffered exhaustion from Hong Kong, South America, and Paris. "Oh, hell." He pulled it open. "What in the world?"

Before him stood a person clad in a black burka. It covered the individual from head to toe, and covered the eyes with a black mesh such that he couldn't even ascertain eye color.

"Excuse me." The figure brushed by him into the entryway.

Crayle thought of a martial response, but couldn't find the energy. Before he could react in any other way, the individual grabbed the material atop its head, and drew off the entire garment. Then, turned to face the host.

A jaw dropped.

Crayle's.

He fought to express just one word.

"Kimbel!"

He shut the door. And rechecked his security app.

Just a taxi cab outside. With blackened windows.

"Who's here?" called Hekka from the living room. "Anyone I know?"

Kimbel Stones took the near speechless man in front of him by the arm, and led him into the main room.

Hekka saw the President of the United States first. "Everyone!"

They all looked.

They all stood.

Micmac, the musician of the group, began humming *Hail To The Chief*.

The president raised his hand.

The former UDT/SEAL tapered off.

"Who is our guest, Magus?" came from the kitchen. The two mothers were in the midst of preparing lunch.

Another reality struck. Crayle punched at his phone. The large, sliding door and window to the million dollar lake view turned a translucent white. No one could see inside. He extended his hand toward the platinum blonde in the kitchen. "Kimbel, this is Hekka's mother, Helmi, and my own mother, Caitrin. Under the circumstances, we can have them represent as diplomats from their native countries, Finland and Wales."

"I'm charmed, ladies. No need for formalities. I'm on first name basis to the team, here. Adding two more is not a problem. You'll have your security clearances by tomorrow."

"We heard Kimbel from the doorway. Is that okay?" Helmi asked.

"I don't believe I spoke that loud." Stones turned to Crayle. "Check for bugs."

Crayle's mother gave a look. "What does he mean by team?"

"Another time, mom."

"And I'll add these three..." He indicated the babies. "...when they're old enough to talk."

"Deal," Crayle agreed. "Okay, add one more for lunch. Micmac can serve as the president's taster."

"If that means I get to eat sooner, done!"

They shared Hekka specialty Serrano burgers plus garlic jalapeno fries, and uncharacteristic banter. Each knew there was far too much if they delved into team or personal subject matter.

When they finished, Stones turned to his host. "Flip on the news, Magus. I need to catch up."

Crayle complied. "Top of the hour. And there's the lead in."

The banner headline caught their attention.

"THE PRESIDENT IS MISSING!"

The president stood. "I suppose I should get back. But first, I didn't just happen by. I made this trip secretly and personally to give my thanks to the team. A special thanks from me and our country. With a special thanks to Phoebe, and to Lenny. I have reserved space for both at Arlington. Is that all right?"

Alona teared up. She nodded. "Yes, Kimbel. But I have a request."

"Please."

"Bury them side-by-side . . . like brother and sister."

Stones glanced over at Micmac.

"Absolutely."

"Then it shall be so ordered. And with that, *hasta la vista*, *au revoir*, see you next time." The president re-donned his disguise frock, and departed.

EPILOGUE

THE ILLUMINÉ

The Illuminé, founded in 1623, as a French-flavored adjunct to the German Illuminati, held that the enlightened elite, as defined by themselves, needed to lead while all others—the masses—followed. The efforts of Sylvain Lalumière and Chin Yao-wu to change the political landscape in France and China, respectively, was to be the initiation of a worldwide movement. The Elder, who happened to be the Prince of Monaco and the intellectual at the top of the heap, had chosen two very dissimilar countries and cultures to get the process down. Then, a rollout of those successes would follow to the remainder of the world's countries. Surely, the detractors would be forced to relent and admit that the enlightened were not merely chosen to lead, but were so destined.

That the unlikely and eclectic Crayle team, working under Jack Sommers, would both enable and defeat the efforts was unconscionable to the intellectual elite. No matter their IQs, like all elitists, they couldn't see past their own eyes. They did change the world. Just not in the manner they'd envisioned They envisioned intellectually elevated monarchs reproducing the intellect by new royal bloodlines.

THE CHINESE

Empress Ling An-yee continued her reign in China unabated. Capable underlings of the leaders killed by the bomb factory explosion took over the day-to-day operations. It turned out they didn't at all like their former bosses and were glad to see them go. They worked for the betterment, not for themselves, of the resurrected Imperial China. In a way, a new beginning. Micmac and his baby daughter moved into sumptuous quarters in the Hong Kong Palace to help in any way he could. Especially with technology and defensive military tactics. Crayle kept in touch with infrequent flights there to supply strategic planning and to ensure proper implementation. And to ensure off-the-books diplomatic communications between Empress Ling and President Stones.

THE GERMANS

The Germans became Germans again. Everything was in order. With the past failed leadership and with the remnants of the Aryan Alliance eliminated in South America, new leaders were chosen by the people. The new leaders saw the disparity between immigrant refugees and the indigenous Germanic peoples, and placed no blame. They offered fully-compensated repatriation and, with peace and prosperity having pervaded their homelands, the offers were universally accepted. The displaced people could return to familiar cultures, and to their now quite safe environment. To keep the progress in place, the Germans initiated trade agreements and utilized other methods to insure the financial well-being of those countries. For those who were skeptical, dual citizenship sealed the deal.

THE FRENCH

In less than a day, the new king and queen of France became a blip on the pages of history. But the notion of a special, bloodline-oriented leadership had taken hold. All of that set in motion by the revival of The Man In The Iron Mask. The acronymic Mitim had brought that to be. The Crown Prince, also for less than a day, became king. The new monarch required commensurate excellent food and fine wine. In La Belle France, not a problem. What was needed, however, was a wife for the new king, and offspring for France's future. There was good news on that front. The Queen of Sweden would be happy to oblige.

THE FRENCHMAN

Jean-Marc Lalumière. From bastard son of his now-deceased father and mother, Sylvain and Épiphanie, to King of France. It had been a long run. And part with morally-challenged and psychopathic Pattie Norbrunn. He took a moment to count his blessings that he hadn't become a member of the CIA rogue operative's extensive graveyard registry.

THE SWEDES

They were not quite sure what to make of the their queen running off to Paris and marrying the new French king. What worried them most was the possible outcome that Sweden would be annexed to France as its northernmost region, and that the chefs down south would have no clue on how to properly prepare Swedish meatballs or how to include delicious, healthy Lingonberries in their diets.

THE VATICAN

The Vatican wasted no time to replace its nuncio delegate to Chile. Especially after America's CIA informed their newest major asset, the pope, that said nuncio had worked in concert with the Aryan chief in South America. Shades of the post-WWII Vatican, which helped NAZI war criminals escape to Argentina, was one the pope intended to put back to bed. Post haste. The fact that the nuncio had acquired one of the mini-nuke devices and spirited it to target either the Vatican or Israel was kept where it belonged. Under wraps.

THE AMERICANS

The visit of Crayle and Micmac to Hanford, Washington's nuclear reactor site had produced heady intel. It enabled the two to travel Hong Kong and, by remote control of an underground nuclear weapon production site, to destroy the mini-nuke proliferation capability, and, at the same time, the evil leftovers of the previous Chinese communist regime. In so doing, President Stones' covert crew eliminated the manufacture of miniaturized nuclear devices in China and, subsequently, their distribution worldwide. The world became a far safer place. The Crayle team later hooked up the Stones State Department with Empress Ling in China and the new French king to set up fabulous trade agreements beneficial to all parties involved. He did have to think twice about rewarding the team members with any more vacations gone wrong. He'd have a talk with Darryl. Over a Molson's Canadian with a shot of Canadian Club tossed in.

THE CRAYLES

They continued taking a breather back at the Big Bear cabin with baby Kianna. They considered turning in their non-existent quasi-CIA badges, and retiring from the world of geopolitical intrigues and plain old spying. Best to enjoy life and all that meant as long as you were alive.

THE CRAYLES—GOLDENEYE

Hekka had been holding a secret that she finally shared with her husband. She'd arranged for a little vacation week down in the Caribbean. It wasn't until they landed, that she told him the destination. He'd kidded about someday spending some quiet time at the former residence of prolific and iconic spy novelist, Ian Fleming. And there it was. One full week at *Goldeneye*. He said 'Thanks' in every way he could think of.

ME

Done. The sequence of seven novels of my International Thriller Series is now complete. I've earned a break. Hmmm. How about a week at *Goldeneye*?

Series End

ABOUT THE AUTHOR

Committed to international affairs, political intrigue and espionage novelist Dennis Bowen has researched his stories in more than 70 countries. That Bowen engenders realism and spice in his thrillers due to his wartime service, and his defense and intelligence community background, led one reader to remark, "Bowen knows his stuff." *The Jasmine Negative* follows *The Water Diamonds*, *The Blackstone Perfection*, *The Crystal Seduction*, *The Redrock Quarantine, The Final Masquerade,* and *The Virtue Transition* as Book 7 in his International Thriller Series. When not traveling the globe to research his next thriller, he resides on the Southern California coast.

Facebook: http://www.facebook.com/DennisBowenThrillers/
Twitter: http://www.twitter.com/DBowenThrillers/
Website: http://www.dennisbowen.com/

AUTHOR'S NOTE

I hope you enjoyed ***The Jasmine Negative***. As is evident from the cover, this is Book 7 of the ***International Thriller Series***. And, it is likely the last in the series. The initial section of this note explains, in brief, the process I followed from beginning to end. I decided to include it because there are interesting insights for both readers and aspiring authors.

In the second section of the Author's Note, I chose to do something groundbreaking. To recommend alternative modes of reading, especially for novels such as mine that provide plenty of character dialog, but without extensive author narratives. I've discovered different approaches to the process that can provide additional enjoyment for my readers. That should raise a question in your mind. You learned to read in school and likely have successfully read several novels, including this one. Isn't there a standard process for reading? The simple answer is Yes. However, there are a couple of alternatives that may not occur to everyone, especially adults. But first, here are a few words regarding how this writing of novels began, and carried through to the end.

• • •

How did this sequential series of seven come to be? Prior to my initial writing effort, I would go for bicycle rides around a lake. It was a self-imposed prescription for exercise, fresh air, and a mental time out. Ideas for a story would just pop into my head without any solicitation whatsoever. I'd return home and write them in a notebook. By 2011, I decided to write a novel. The plot would demonstrate how the geopolitical landscape could be severely modified by evil-intentioned malefactors using miniature nuclear devices. I decided to write all the stories in long hand to keep myself physically connected, versus the technological mental distancing inherent with using a computer. After substantial scribblings, annotations, and cross-outs, the words did find their way into the digital orchestration.

Notes on the characters, locations, and scenes grew and grew. I attended a few writers' conferences, read several books, and decided to put pen to paper. So I did. My original estimate, however, would produce a novel of about 750 pages. Too big. I divided the story into three successive novels to make it more manageable, and to provide the initial product to readers much faster.

After three months of putting pen to paper, I realized through epiphany that I'd really gotten to know the story, the settings, and the characters. In fact, I knew the latter so well, I could just keep a mental eye on them, and they could write the scenes. The good news was they couldn't charge me for their efforts. And better yet, I could take all the credit.

As I wrote the three novels, ideas kept coming. By the time I finished them, I had enough notes for two more. Okay, I said. It was meant to be a five novel series. By the time I completed the fifth story, I had notes for two more. The trend led me to pronounce, on more than one occasion, the famous line from the Peanuts cartoon series: Charlie Brown saying, "Good grief!" Or words to that effect. I also considered giving up bicycle riding.

With ***The Jasmine Negative***, I feel I have completed the series. Done.

Still, a quite knowledgeable individual whose judgment I trust, and who is deeply familiar with the stories and characters, has intimated that there just might be an eighth novel required.

I say again. "Good grief!"

• • •

Who would write a segment to readers on how to read a novel?

I would.

I've read many, many geopolitical spy thriller tomes over the years, most of which have followed a very similar, industry-wide format. There are even books about the proper way to write a story, which seems to fly in the face of creativity.

I have read, and continue to read, the standard fare. But I have found, as I suppose other readers have found, one grows a bit weary and launches into speed reading mode, lest one fall asleep. I can scoot over much of the author narrative, not lose much of the story line, and increase the pace substantially.

I assure you, no writer in this genre spends the countless hours writing and perfecting their stories as a cure for insomnia. When I set out on this endeavor, I promised myself I would seek to write what are referred to in the business as tight novels. Substance moving quickly. My own style is to write tight novels and try to keep myself off the stage. The stage is for the characters, not the author. At least, that's been my approach. So I don't spend time informing the reader with detail such as *the woman moved her middle finger a millimeter to the left*. It's a tough choice when everyone expects a three or four inch thick novel in my genre, but I seek to avoid overwriting the stories.

So I ended up saving forests and planets and feel real good about myself. But there's more.

I discovered that at least with my own stories, reading them out loud produced even more satisfaction. Let me explain.

Speed reading tight novels can cause one to skip over critical aspects of the story and miss key details. And 'the feel' can get lost. Reading out loud slows the reader down. Since my books are understandably more concise than the standard fare, reading them in this fashion takes about the same amount of time.

And yet, I've discovered a third mode. Once you get a feel for the characters, don't just read the dialogs out loud, but play the parts. Become the actors in the movie. This can add significantly to your reading pleasure. It might even bring a smile regarding your heretofore undiscovered talent. And since I didn't include every obscure, minute detail of the fictional characters, individual readers can interpret and put their own take on them in the dialogs.

Some, including myself, find that in re-reading any of the ***International Thriller Series*** novels, a reader can enjoy them just as much, or even enjoy them more. You can still get everything in normal, silent reading mode, but I suggest you return to a favorite chapter in this story, read it out loud, visualize the characters and observe the difference.

I do perform a great deal of international research since that is the forum in which my stories take place. Although I plan to finally take a little time off, the ideas never stop coming. Fortunately, I did start a second series I called ***The Backstory Files*** in which I took a second-tier individual from the first series and provided how the title character, ***STONES***, transitioned from a National Security Agency operative to Vice President of the United States in an intense, brief period of time. I have many more characters for which I can write thriller back stories.

And with that, best wishes to all those who've supported my efforts, to all those in foreign lands that have provided precious local flavor intel, and finally to every reader on the entire planet. You are why we do this. Seriously. Thank you.

—Dennis Bowen